Assigned to Protect
Danger in Destiny
Book 7

Melanie D. Snitker

DALLIONE MEDIA, LLC

Assigned to Protect
Danger in Destiny: Book 7
By Melanie D. Snitker

Dallionz Media, LLC
P.O. Box 5283
Abilene, TX 79608

Cover Art: Dallionz Media, LLC

Melanie D. Snitker
melanie@melaniedsnitker.com
www.melaniedsnitker.com

This is a work of fiction. Names, characters, businesses, places, events, and incidents either are the products of the author's imagination or used in a fictitious manner. Any resemblance to actual persons, living or dead, or actual events is purely coincidental.

Chapter One

Police Officer Jenny Durant opened every stall door until she was certain the restroom was empty. This particular one was reserved for individuals at the courthouse waiting to testify. Even though it shouldn't be as frequented as the more public restrooms, Jenny wasn't about to allow their witness inside without making sure it was safe.

With it cleared, she exited to find FBI Agent Blake Patterson waiting with their witness.

Annie Grassle shot Jenny an annoyed look before brushing past to disappear behind the heavy wooden door.

Jenny shifted to stand in front of the door to make sure no one else entered the restroom. She'd dealt with many interesting and even frustrating people during her time with the Destiny Police Department. She considered herself to be a patient person and would like to think any of her fellow officers would agree with that. So why did Grassle consistently rub her the wrong way?

She and Blake had been tasked to protect her until today, when she was scheduled to give her testimony that would hopefully lead to the conviction of a local judge. The judge was being charged with jury tampering and bribery in order to keep a suspect out of jail. It wasn't the judge himself that they worried about, but rather the suspect's ties to a drug cartel that was well-known for eliminating anyone who got in its way.

Since public corruption was one of the FBI's top criminal investigative priorities, they sent an agent—Blake—to assist local law enforcement in protecting Grassle and making sure the judge was put behind bars.

Once Grassle gave her testimony, she'd be whisked into the Federal Witness Security (WITSEC) program, where she'd disappear with a new identity. A new life.

And Jenny could go on to a new assignment.

"You really don't like her, do you?"

Blake's voice, somehow still deep even though he spoke just above a whisper, drew her attention. His hazel eyes glittered with amusement even as he kept up his constant scan of the hallway.

"Can you honestly say you do?" Jenny straightened her spine. "I'll be glad when this assignment is over."

It'd been five grueling days of making sure Grassle stayed safe and lived to give her testimony. Working with Blake made it that much more difficult. At the time, it'd taken everything in her not to ask Chief Dolman for a different assignment.

Blake seemed to enjoy pushing her buttons. He was good at his job—there was no doubt about that. They'd had a similar assignment a year ago, and although it'd lasted less than forty-eight hours, it was long enough for Jenny to know the guy was as sure of himself as he was handsome. Most people seemed to find him humorous, but she usually categorized the guy as mildly infuriating.

As annoying as it was to have him constantly critique everything about her, he was far from annoying to look at. He stood at nearly six feet tall with dark hair and a neatly trimmed goatee and mustache. He exuded confidence from the way he moved to the way he took command of a situation. Yet another trait that was more appealing than it was off-putting.

It'd be easier if she could ignore the guy completely, but he had one of those winning smiles that somehow coaxed a matching one from almost anyone he spoke with. Except for maybe her, not that he didn't try. Resisting giving him the reactions he seemed so intent on getting was a full-time job —a distracting one, and she couldn't afford any distractions.

The whole situation bothered her because she normally got along with almost everyone, and on this assignment, she found herself aggravated with them both.

Blake ran a hand over his strong chin. "I'll be glad when we can hand her over to WITSEC, too."

His admission surprised Jenny. If he'd been frustrated with Grassle, he hadn't shown it.

Technically speaking, protecting Grassle hadn't been all that difficult. She'd pretty much stayed at the hotel until today—not that she'd been happy about it. It was listening to the woman complain and grumble for hours a day that had taken its toll. Jenny all but rejoiced when the night shift took over.

Still, there was satisfaction in knowing that they'd kept her safe and that her testimony would hopefully lead to getting dangerous individuals off the streets.

A court clerk stepped into the hall and motioned toward Blake. "We'll be ready for Ms. Grassle momentarily." He gave them a friendly smile.

Blake gave him a nod. "Thank you."

Jenny pushed the restroom door open. "Ms. Grassle? It's time to go."

"Yep." The single word echoed in the empty room, quickly followed by a toilet flushing. A minute later, Grassle appeared and, for the first time, seemed nervous. Her gaze darted up and down the hallway as she ran the palms of her hands down her slacks and straightened her blouse. "Let's get this over with."

A wave of sympathy washed over Jenny. She could imagine how stressful this situation would be. Granted, she'd never accepted a bribe as a juror, but she'd had to testify in many court proceedings. They never got easier.

She considered offering some encouragement but knew Grassle would only counter it with snark, so she kept her mouth shut.

Blake shifted to Grassle's left while Jenny took her right. Together, they escorted her to where the court clerk waited for them.

"This way, please." He led them down the hall past one courtroom.

When they neared a second one, goose bumps peppered Jenny's arms. She glanced behind them.

Blake, who never seemed to miss a detail, looked over at her and slowed. "What is it?"

"I'm not sure." She turned around to look behind them. It was impossible to pinpoint the source of the feeling except that it was oppressive, and she couldn't quite shake it.

There was no time to analyze it before a deafening roar was immediately followed by a surge of pressure that shoved Jenny forward. She crashed to the ground with enough force to drive the air from her lungs. Bits of debris landed on her arms and the backs of her hands that were protecting her head.

The world seemed to slow to a crawl. Her lungs ached to draw in a breath. The heat of the air around her, mixed with her throbbing knee and the pressure in her left ear, was almost unbearable.

Blake. Was he okay?

Where was Grassle?

Finally, her lungs expanded, and sweet oxygen filled them as she gasped.

A hand clamped onto her upper arm. She turned her head to find Blake kneeling beside her, one hand on her and another grasping Grassle's elbow. Relief flooded her body knowing they were both alive. His lips moved, but no sound came from them.

Everything around her was muted. People were scrambling in the hallway, but she couldn't hear it. Smoke hovered near the ceiling, partially concealing the strobing lights that accompanied the fire alarm.

She moved to get her feet underneath her and then stood with Blake's help. The cacophony of chaos around them started to filter through—the noise louder in her right ear—and she winced.

"Durant! Can you hear me? Are you hurt?"

Blake still hadn't released her arm, and Jenny felt unsteady enough that she was thankful for the extra support.

She shook her head. "I'm okay." The door to the courtroom they'd been just outside of was mangled, the doorframe singed. "A bomb?"

Blake gave a grim nod. He tilted his head toward Grassle. "We need to get her to a safe location."

As much as Jenny wanted to help those around her, he was right. It was impossible to tell how much damage was caused by the explosion. They were on the second floor of the courthouse. Had the integrity of the building been compromised? There might even be more than one bomb. Scenarios played through Jenny's mind, but they had to take things one step at a time.

Blake dropped his hand, and Jenny moved to put hers on Grassle's other shoulder. She spoke into her radio. "This is Durant at the courthouse. There's been an explosion. I repeat, there's been an explosion at the courthouse. Patterson and I are attempting to evacuate the building and get our witness to safety."

"A response unit is on the way. Additional units will be waiting for you at the back entrance."

"Understood." She exchanged another look with Blake.

He immediately went into action. "This way."

Chapter Two

Blake didn't like their current situation. At all. He had a witness to protect, a building full of panicked people, an explosion that he didn't know the extent of, and a partner he suspected may have been injured in the blast.

Jenny was closer to the explosion than he had been. Judging from his own aches and scrapes, he imagined she felt worse. She was speaking loudly, too, which meant her hearing may have been compromised. A blast like the one they'd just been exposed to could result in damage to one or both of her ears.

They needed to get out of this building, get Grassle to safety, and then he had every intention of making sure Jenny was seen by an EMT.

Together, he and Jenny worked to shield Grassle as they made their way to the stairwell. It was filled with people pushing against each other in their hurry to get as far away from the explosion as possible. Courthouse security reminded people to make their way to the exits and to remain calm.

Doing their best to avoid everyone else, Jenny, Blake, and Grassle skipped steps to reach the ground floor. Jenny led the way, hugging the rail with Grassle behind her. Blake came in last, his attention shifting between the women in front of him and the individuals around them.

Right now, he could only guess at the purpose behind the explosion. Was it meant to kill someone specific or to only stall a trial? Perhaps it was a random act of violence, but his heart rate picked up at the thought that maybe all of this was done to flush people out in a panic so Grassle could be abducted more easily. They had to get her out of there.

Until they knew more, Blake had to assume that whoever set the bomb was after his witness.

They burst through the door onto the first floor and turned right toward the back entrance. Almost everyone else went for the closer front entrance, making it easier to jog down the hallway.

They hadn't even reached the door before it burst open, and several officers entered. Blake recognized Officers Baker and Carrington from the Destiny PD.

Baker immediately put a hand on Grassle's back. "We've been ordered to take the witness in for medical care and to cover the situation until you can both be evaluated by the EMTs."

The words were spoken as they all pushed through the back door and into the bright parking lot beyond. They whisked Grassle away. Anyone else exiting the building was escorted to a safe distance in case the earlier explosion wasn't the only one.

Jenny turned her head and for the first time, Blake got a good look at her left ear. Blood dribbled down from it to her jaw and onto her neck. He put an arm around her shoulders and turned her toward several ambulances that had been stationed nearby.

She tilted her chin up to look at him, confusion on her face. "We don't have to hurry. I'm okay." She lifted her arms and examined the multiple small cuts and scrapes that she could see through the tears in her long-sleeved shirt. "Nothing serious."

Blake stopped walking and pulled a clean handkerchief from his back pocket. He carefully swept some of her long, dark hair away and placed the handkerchief against her left ear, then pulled it away again to show her the small amount of blood that had already soaked into the fabric.

"We need to get that ear checked out."

With a wince followed by a nod, she didn't object when he continued their trek to the ambulances.

An EMT spotted them immediately and ushered them both to sit down on the bumper of the ambulance. Whitman was written on the name tag stitched to the front of his jacket.

"How close were you to the explosion?" The EMT carefully touched Jenny's ear.

She set her jaw, but it was clear the probing was causing her pain.

Blake placed his hand on her shoulder and gave it a supportive squeeze. "We were in the hallway outside the courtroom where I believe the explosion may have originated. Officer Durant here was closest to the blast."

"I see." The EMT leaned back a bit. "My name is Curtis, and I'm going to take a look at your injuries and decide whether you should be transported to the hospital for further testing."

Jenny immediately shook her head. "I'm fine. We need

to check in with our chief and see what else we can do. Make sure all our people made it out of the building."

If there was one thing Blake had always admired about her, it was her determination. It's what made her so good at her job. It's also what had made her so attractive the first time he met her and probably why she seemed unwilling to see him as more than an annoying colleague she was forced to work with.

Not that he'd made it easy on her. Once it was clear she didn't like him, he'd made it his mission to get a reaction out of her one way or another.

He ignored the guilt that tried to wiggle its way to the surface. She could've been killed back there, and the thought of losing a partner—no matter who that was—was completely unacceptable. If her injuries didn't prevent her from continuing with their assignment, he had every intention of taking it easy on her in the future. Well, easier, anyway.

Curtis gave Jenny a kind smile. "I sincerely hope that will be the case. I also happen to know that Chief Dolman would have my hide if I sent one of his officers back into the field without doing everything I could to make sure she was fit to do so."

She nodded, giving him permission to continue the examination.

Blake watched as the EMT used an otoscope to look inside her ear.

"The good news is, there's no perforation to your eardrum. The blood we're seeing is from a cut and doesn't originate from the canal." Curtis took an alcohol swab and carefully cleaned away the blood. "You could do with a stitch or two, but I can close this up with a butterfly bandage for now."

"Please do." She chuckled. "I have four brothers. A scar from an explosion would score me some major cool points."

Curtis laughed. "Nice. Can you hear clearly? Are you feeling dizzy?"

Jenny hesitated. "I'm not dizzy. Honestly, I couldn't hear a thing right after the explosion, especially from that ear. It's already a lot better and seems to be improving steadily."

"That's a good sign. If anything changes, you need to be seen by a doctor immediately. Otherwise, your hearing should return over time."

She nodded, a look of relief on her face.

Knowing that Jenny's inner ear hadn't been damaged, coupled with the amused smile on her face, brought Blake an odd mix of relief and an intense need to protect her from anything else that might cause her harm.

He told himself the instinct wasn't any different than how he felt about a witness he'd been charged to protect or anyone else he'd been partnered with.

Not true, but he refused to analyze the why.

He waited as Curtis finished bandaging the wound on her ear and cleaned a couple of larger scrapes on her arms and the backs of her hands. The EMT verified that she hadn't hit her head and then turned his attention to Blake.

"What about you?"

Blake held up his own arms, the sleeves of his shirt torn in several places. "Just a few nicks and scrapes. Nothing to worry about."

"No reduction in your hearing or dizziness?"

"Nothing like that."

Jenny lifted a hand to the bandage on her ear and focused on Blake. "You sure?"

The flicker of concern in her brown eyes meant more

than it should have. He gave her a reassuring smile. "I'm positive. I'm fine."

She studied him for another moment, then gave a satisfied nod. She looked like she might have said something when her attention shifted. Her expression became serious, and she immediately straightened her back.

Blake turned to find Chief Dolman approaching, determination written in his stride.

"Are you both okay?" He looked first at Blake and then focused on Jenny.

"No serious injuries, sir," she reported.

The EMT gave Chief Dolman a nod of confirmation.

"I'm glad to hear it."

"Did all of our people get out okay?" The question came from Jenny.

"They did," Dolman confirmed.

Blake moved to stand next to her. "How's the witness?"

"She's being examined by a doctor and will return to the hotel shortly. Other officers will cover your shift today if you need time to recover, and we can evaluate whether you are able to return to your assignment tomorrow morning. It's unclear when the trial will recommence." He looked at the nearby building. "The courthouse was busy today with several trials taking place. There were three fatalities, multiple injuries, and one suspect is missing. The entire situation is an absolute mess."

"What can we do, Chief?" Jenny squared her shoulders. "Seems like you could use all hands on deck this evening."

Blake agreed completely. The last thing he wanted was to be sidelined. "I'd like to help in any way I can."

Chief Dolman seemed satisfied with their responses. "There'll be a debrief at the station in an hour. I'll see you both there."

With that, the chief strode away, and Curtis rushed to help someone else who needed assistance, leaving Blake and Jenny on their own.

Jenny swept some of her long, wavy hair away from her face, and Blake's gaze caught on the bandage hugging the edge of her left ear. There was no need to voice how fortunate they were to walk away from the blast. He thought about the three people who didn't, and his mood turned dark.

Whoever set the bomb was still out there, and it was impossible to know whether the explosion had accomplished the bomber's goal or if this was just the beginning.

Chapter Three

I f it weren't for the open suitcase on the small desk and the can of Coke on the side table, Jenny wouldn't have believed that Blake was even staying in the hotel room. It was spotless. Did the guy even sleep in the bed at night?

She'd noticed a do-not-disturb sign on the door when they came in, so it wasn't like room service was making the bed for him. She made her bed, too, but it never looked this good.

She raised her voice a little and directed it toward the closed door of the bathroom. "Are you ex-military?"

"Nope. My dad was." His voice was slightly muffled behind the door.

His clothing had suffered numerous small tears in the blast, as had Jenny's. They decided to stop by his hotel so he could change before going back to the station where she had spare clothes waiting.

A minute later, the door opened, and Blake emerged. He'd traded his tan slacks and button-down shirt for a pair of blue jeans and a long-sleeved pullover shirt. The shirt was dark green and accentuated the matching flecks in his hazel eyes. She realized she was staring when his brows drew together in concern.

"Jenny? Are you sure you're okay?"

Warmth flooded her face. Thankfully, he mistook her momentary lapse in common sense for discomfort or pain. She really needed to get a hold of herself.

"Sorry. Yeah." She thought back to their previous conversation and tried to focus. "So, your dad. Did he run a tight ship?"

Blake started to pull items from the pockets of his old pants and transfer them to his jeans. "Yes and no. I was an only child, and my parents never had a happy marriage. They divorced when I was six. From that point on, they shared custody and barely spoke to each other. When I was with my dad, he was strict. Said he had to be to offset my mom, who was pretty hands-off. Honestly, it wouldn't work for most kids, but I made it out okay. For the most part."

There was something in his voice that made Jenny wonder if he was holding something back.

He dropped his damaged clothing into a wastebasket that was barely big enough to hold them. One of the pants legs draped over the side. He picked up a jacket and motioned for her to precede him out of the hotel room. "What about you? Four brothers?" He gave an appreciative whistle. "I can't even imagine."

Jenny shrugged, acutely aware of the ache in her shoulders and neck. Ibuprofen was going to be her friend for the next few days. "Two older brothers, two younger. I have an older sister, too. When you grow up in a big family, you don't really know the difference."

"Do they all live in Destiny? Are you guys close?" He

opened the driver's side of her police car for her before going around to the other side.

She started the car and pulled away from the hotel. "My parents are local, along with one of my brothers. The others are all over Texas. And yeah, we're a tight-knit family."

"That's great." There was a hint of longing in his voice.

Jenny could practically feel his curiosity as they continued the drive in silence. As they got closer, the weight of what happened at the courthouse grew heavier.

She parked and released her seat belt. Before she could get out of the car, Blake put a hand on her arm and shifted to face her.

"Do you believe in God?"

Her eyebrows rose. Of all the things he might have asked her, she hadn't expected this. "Yes. I'm a Christian. I absolutely believe in God." She tilted her head slightly. "Why do you ask?"

"Back at the courthouse, something stopped you in the hallway. If you hadn't hesitated when you did, and we'd been right in front of that doorway..." His voice faltered. "I'm a Christian, too, and I don't put much stock in coincidences."

Goose bumps pebbled along her arms, and her heart stuttered.

"Neither do I." For a moment, she allowed herself to consider an alternative ending to earlier events before shutting the possibilities out of her mind. "I'm thankful He got us out of there in one piece."

Blake gave her arm a squeeze, nodded once, and opened his door.

Inside the precinct, Jenny led the way to the largest conference room. It was already half full. Several of her fellow officers greeted her with hugs and voiced their relief that she and Blake were okay.

There were windows all along one wall. Against another, someone had set up several tables laden with sandwiches, chips, sodas, and two big pots of coffee—neither of which was decaffeinated.

No doubt all of this was thanks to Tia Warner. She worked in dispatch, made the best coffee Jenny had ever tasted, and somehow managed to keep a finger on the pulse of the department. If someone was sick or having difficulties outside of work, Tia knew it and did everything she could to help.

Jenny turned to Blake. "I'm going to go change. I'll be back in a flash."

Without waiting for him to respond, she left the room.

She'd been wearing plainclothes while on this latest assignment but opted for her uniform for the rest of the day. By the time she got back, the conference room was even busier. Chief Dolman had arrived as well.

She scanned the room to find Blake sitting at one end of the table, a sandwich and a cup of coffee in front of him. He tilted his head toward the chair beside him where another cup of coffee waited for her.

Her knee ached as she took a seat. Pushing away the memory of being thrown to the ground during the explosion, she took a sip of the coffee and nodded her approval. Apparently, Blake had been paying attention because it was exactly the way she liked it. She had no idea he'd even noticed.

"Thank you."

"You're welcome. I would've grabbed a sandwich for you, but I wasn't sure which kind you would want."

Jenny was about to tell him that she'd get one later

when someone put an arm around her shoulders. She swiveled her chair to look up at her friend and fellow officer, Detective Nate Walker.

"Hey, I was relieved to hear you're okay." His gaze swept over her face as though he were reassuring himself that she wasn't seriously injured. "I knew you were at the courthouse when we got word of the explosion."

"It was scary, but I'm fine. We're fine." She pushed her chair away from the table far enough to motion toward Blake. "This is Agent Blake Patterson. My partner on this latest assignment. Blake, this is Detective Nate Walker."

Nate had been out on vacation the last few days, so he hadn't had the opportunity to meet Blake earlier.

The men shook hands and exchanged pleasantries.

Nate patted her on the shoulder. "Have you eaten yet?"

"Not yet."

"Stay here. I'll go grab something for you."

Minutes later, he returned with a turkey and cheddar sandwich and a bag of barbecue chips.

"Thanks, Nate."

"No problem. Depending on how today goes, we may have to cancel dinner tonight."

She had a feeling that was exactly what they'd have to do. "There's always next week if that's the case."

Nate headed back to the sandwich table, and Jenny turned to find Blake watching her, one eyebrow raised. It was clear one of his sarcastic comments was right on the tip of his tongue.

"Nate's a friend, and so is his fiancée, Bailey. The three of us meet for dinner once a month or so. Not that it's any of your business." She opened the bag of chips with a pop and placed one on her tongue, the tangy barbecue seasoning a welcome taste.

"So, not your boyfriend, then."

He was baiting her, and she wasn't about to bite. Instead, she aimed a side kick to his shin.

His only response was a low chuckle.

Chief Dolman cleared his throat and asked everyone to take a seat. Blake was immediately all business. It was one thing Jenny could appreciate about him—at least he knew when to back off on the clowning around and stupid comments.

The room quieted as all attention focused on the chief. At just over six feet tall with wide shoulders and a commanding presence, he was a force to be reckoned with. Especially when his gray eyes held the determination they did now. He scratched at his hairline where his dark hair faded to gray.

"We've got a complex investigation on our hands. The sooner we can get the loose ends tied up, the better off we'll be. Our priority is to determine who set the bomb at the courthouse and who the target might have been." Chief Dolman gave a nod to Officer Philip Lorenzo, a member of Destiny PD's bomb squad.

Lorenzo stood. "Preliminary investigation has revealed the bomb was placed in a trash can just inside Courtroom D. It was activated remotely. We're going over the remaining pieces and looking for anything unusual. See if that matches up with a signature from another bomb in the system. Meanwhile, there was no structural damage to the courthouse, but between the mess created by the explosion itself and the sprinkler system, it's uncertain how long it'll be before that courtroom is re-opened."

"Unfortunately," the chief added, "all court proceedings that were canceled today will need to be rescheduled and with one less courtroom available."

Jenny knew exactly what that meant. It could be several days or even a week before Grassle would be able to testify. She wasn't sure if Blake would be sticking around, or if he'd be sent back to Austin where he worked at the satellite FBI office. She supposed it would likely depend on his boss and the arrangement made with the chief.

Chief Dolman continued with his updates. "Right now, we have three main cases that may or may not be connected. The explosion claimed the lives of three people, including a lawyer, a defendant who was on trial in the courtroom where the bomb went off, and a court clerk standing in the doorway."

The court clerk... It had to be the man who had been escorting them down the hallway to their own courtroom. His face and friendly smile swam into Jenny's mind, and she swallowed back a wave of sadness. It could have easily been her standing in the doorway instead. Or five seconds later, and they would've all been clear of the actual blast.

The individual who set that bomb off may have had a target in mind, but they clearly didn't care who else might have been caught in the blast.

Chapter Four

Blake sensed Jenny tensing beside him when Chief Dolman mentioned the death of the court clerk. He had no doubt it was the clerk who had come to get them when it was time for Grassle to testify. The sadness over the loss of life was magnified by the fact that Jenny was mere feet from the same fate.

He glanced over at her and saw the moisture in her eyes. His instinct to reassure her by nudging her arm or giving her knee a tap with his own was strong, but he wasn't sure it would be welcome. Instead, he sent up a silent prayer that God would give her strength and peace as the debrief continued.

Detective John Paris, one of the men at Destiny PD that Blake had worked with before, stood after receiving a nod from the chief.

"Joseph Kent was the defendant killed in the explosion. He was a well-known gang member on trial for murdering two rival gang members, as well as an innocent bystander in a drive-by shooting. The rival gang has made it very public that they wanted Kent dead. We can't ignore the possibility that the bomb was set specifically for him today."

Detective Paris tasked two other officers to assist him with that part of the investigation.

Another officer with the last name of Smith on her uniform stood then and addressed the group. "During the chaos after the bombing, another defendant went missing. Marcos Hernandez was on trial for allegedly stealing money from a construction company he managed. There's been no sign of him since. It's also possible that the bombing was meant to be a diversion that allowed Hernandez the opportunity to slip out while everyone else was seeking safety. A member of his detail was found unconscious on the floor with a blow to the head. Tracking Hernandez down is also a high priority."

Detective Walker, the man who'd spoken to Jenny and brought her something to eat, got to his feet. "Finally, we need to explore the possibility that the witness Officer Durant and Agent Patterson were protecting may have been the target. The bomb was detonated remotely, and that meant someone had eyes on the hallway and the room in which the bomb had originally been set. It's possible that it was detonated to prevent the witness from testifying." He looked directly at Jenny. "Until we know for sure, extra precaution needs to be taken. If the witness was the target, then the attempt failed. We can't ignore the possibility that another effort may be made."

Blake clenched his jaw. Walker wasn't wrong. It could be days before Grassle finally got to give her testimony and safely enter WITSEC. Until then, they needed to be extra vigilant.

Over the following twenty minutes, officers were given specific jobs to do or angles to research. Once dismissed, those who hadn't eaten grabbed a sandwich before getting back to work.

Chief Dolman caught Jenny's attention and asked her and Blake to stay behind. When the conference room had cleared out, Dolman leaned against the edge of the large table.

"If you're both certain you're okay to return to duty, I'd like you to resume your posts protecting the witness first thing tomorrow morning. Extra units will be positioned throughout the hotel." He looked at Jenny. "The likelihood that this case is tied up before the weekend is small. I'll make sure you still have Saturday off for your brother's wedding."

"I appreciate that, Chief. Thank you. And as far as working tomorrow, that won't be a problem. I hope you'll put me to good use today in the meantime."

"Same, sir," Blake agreed. "I'll be speaking with my SSA this evening and updating him on the situation. If there's anything else the agency can do to help, please let me know."

"Check in with Officer Smith. See if you can help locate Hernandez. The more boots on the ground, the better."

With that, they were dismissed.

They found Smith on the far side of the bullpen where she was giving out assignments. "I can't imagine Hernandez would go back to the construction company he stole from, but we need to cover our bases." She asked one of the officers to head over and see if their missing defendant had shown his face there.

Officer Smith noticed them and stopped. "Durant, good to see you and Agent Patterson are okay. Is there something I can do for you?"

"Actually, the chief said we are on loan for the afternoon. So what can *we* do for *you*?"

"Fabulous." She used her phone for a moment. "I just texted you the address of Hernandez's sister here in Destiny. Pay her a visit and find out if she's seen her brother since he escaped from the courthouse. The two were close, so I can see him trying to hide out at her house."

"We can do that." Jenny's phone pinged with the incoming text.

Smith accepted a file from another officer and immediately tucked it under her arm. "Great. Let me know what you find out. Then, keep an eye on the place for a few hours. Let's see if he decides to show up. I'll send someone to swap with you at five this evening."

They were dismissed, and Jenny pivoted and strode across the room on her way out of the precinct. They'd barely stepped foot outside the station when she glanced at Blake over her shoulder. "I can handle this if you have other things to do. You'd mentioned needing to speak with your SSA."

He'd gotten the impression several times that he might not have been her first choice when it came to their assignment to protect Grassle. This was the first time, though, that she'd given him an out. Blake stopped, and it took several steps for Jenny to realize he wasn't walking with her anymore.

She turned to face him and frowned. "What's wrong?"

"Nothing's wrong. I *am* wondering, though, why my partner is trying to ditch me."

Her eyes widened. "I'm not trying to ditch you. I'm simply suggesting that you could take the afternoon and do something else with it if you wanted to."

"And I don't need to. For the record, when I'm assigned

a partner, I take that very seriously. I'm the Gibbs to your DiNozzo until we clock out."

This time, an amused smile lifted the corners of her lips, and a stubborn light lit up her eyes. "I think you have that backward, buddy."

"Nope. Pretty sure I don't." With that, he started walking again and passed her, making it back to her squad car before she did. He opened the driver's door and, with an exaggerated bow, motioned for her to take a seat.

Jenny rolled her eyes before sliding behind the steering wheel.

Blake chuckled to himself as he jogged around the car and got in. "Okay, so update me on Hernandez. Is he considered dangerous?"

"Not from a violent standpoint. Marcos Hernandez worked as the manager for a local construction company for over a decade. The company changed hands last year, and when it did, the new owner started to spot some discrepancies in the books." She paused and listened to something that came over the police radio before continuing. "The new owner quietly hired someone to go through the financial records and discovered that Hernandez had been purchasing items for the construction company that never actually made it to the yard. It started out as a can of paint here, some lumber there. But as time went on, he became more and more bold."

"How much did he siphon out that way?"

"Nearly six million over the course of ten years."

Blake gave a long whistle. "And he'd have gotten away with it, too, if it weren't for that meddling new owner and his pesky dog."

"Exactly." Jenny turned off Twelfth Street and onto Buckeye Avenue. "The thing is, the guy is as slimy as it gets.

But violent? I can't see it. I think he took advantage of the situation and made a run for it."

"How close is he with his sister?" He glanced at the text that Jenny forwarded him from Officer Smith. "Kelly Rodriguez."

"They're very close. According to Kelly, her kids love their Uncle Marcos. She's a single mom, and Hernandez took the boys to baseball practice and things like that." She glanced at Blake as they pulled to a stop in front of a one-story house set away from the street. It was in desperate need of a new coat of paint, but the lawn was cut and the flower beds tidy. "I'm not saying he wasn't a crook. I mean, the guy stole a lot of money. But agreeing to a bomb that could potentially kill a bunch of innocent people? I don't think so."

From what she'd said, he was inclined to agree. Then again, desperate people were often capable of doing desperate things—things they would never do normally.

Chapter Five

Kelly Rodriguez sat with her arms crossed tightly in front of her and her back straight as a board. She wasn't exactly welcoming when she found them on her doorstep but she had invited them in. Was she hiding something and afraid they'd find out? Or was she upset about her brother and annoyed that she had to answer questions regarding something she didn't have any information about?

Jenny perched on the edge of the worn brown couch. It was one of three matching pieces of furniture in the small living room. The house was older—probably built in the 1970s. Even though there were a lot of things that needed to be updated, the home was clean. Organized.

Even the two young children building with blocks on the floor had been polite when they arrived. The little boys had obeyed instantly when their mother suggested they go play in their room.

Blake leaned into the back of the couch, his posture relaxed, his expression open. "Here's the thing, Ms. Rodriguez. We don't think your brother had anything to do with the bomb. But unfortunately, he's missing, and there are people out there drawing conclusions. He will get caught eventually, and it's better if he turns himself in. Detective Durant and I were both there during the explosion. Trust us, it was confusing and chaotic. Maybe your brother ran because he was afraid there would be another explosion."

Obviously, Hernandez had plenty of time to turn himself in since then, but Blake's approach was slowly chipping away at some of Ms. Rodriguez's defenses.

Jenny tried to make herself relax like Blake. She crossed one leg over the other, and it took everything in her not to wince at the ache and sharp pain in her knee. After the fall she took during the blast, she suspected it would be good and bruised by tomorrow.

Judging by the quick glance Blake threw her way, he'd noticed her discomfort. Well, she could never accuse the FBI agent of not being observant.

Jenny offered Ms. Rodriguez what she hoped was an encouraging smile. "I have four brothers, and I totally know what it's like. They'll drive you absolutely crazy, but I can't imagine not having them in my life."

Ms. Rodriguez nodded, her eyes glittering with unshed tears. "Do you have children?"

"No, I don't."

"I have four kids that I've been raising all on my own. Or I would be if it weren't for Marcos. I don't know how I'm going to do this now." A lone tear finally forced its way through her defenses, and she swiped it away. "I can't imagine him doing something that's only going to add to his time served."

Blake cleared his throat. "Do you have any idea where he might have gone?"

"No. He hasn't come here, and this is the only place I can think of." Her gaze darted to the door and back. So fast, Jenny almost missed it. Was she worried someone was going to stop by, or was she wishing they would leave?

Blake exchanged a glance with her, and his opinion was clear. There wasn't much else they were going to get from the defendant's sister.

Jenny reached for one of her cards and handed it over. "If he comes by, or if you hear from him, please let me know. Or ask him to call in."

Ms. Rodriguez took the card but gave no indication of what she might be thinking. She stood and escorted them to the door. "I'd appreciate you letting me know if you find him."

"Of course."

With that, they took their leave. They'd barely turned their backs to the house when the door closed, and the lock slipped into place behind them.

They said nothing until they were back in the Jenny's car and pulling away from the curb.

Jenny turned right to drive around the block and park across the street and two houses down from the Rodriquez home. It was close enough to see anyone coming or going but not so close to draw suspicion. "I don't think she'll call us if he does show up."

"I tend to agree with you." Blake removed his seat belt. "I can't say I blame her, at least not entirely. It sounds like she and the kids depend on him a lot."

"Yeah, it does. It's a shame he had to go and get himself arrested. I mean, he had to know it would happen eventually." The sad thing was, if Martinez had stopped at a million dollars, or even two, and then left the company to find another job, he might have gotten away with it. He'd gotten greedy. Like most crimes, it came back to bite not just him but his extended family as well.

They sat in silence for several minutes before Blake tapped the clock face. "We should've brought stakeout food. Some snacks to get us through. Something to drink." He turned partway in his seat and looked out the window. "Too bad there's not a convenience store nearby."

Jenny pointed to the bottle of soda he'd brought with him. "I think you're covered with something to drink. As far as snacks go, we just ate. We're going to be here for less than four hours before Smith sends the other unit to take over. We're not going to starve to death."

"It's not strictly about eating because you're hungry. It's about having snacks that you wouldn't eat otherwise. Like when you go on a road trip. Snacks help pass the time. Please tell me you know what I'm talking about."

Blake was looking at her with such astonishment that Jenny couldn't help but laugh.

"Of course, I *normally* buy road trip and stakeout food." She followed suit and released her seat belt so she could be a little more comfortable. Between the laptop and radio, though, there wasn't a whole lot of extra room. "So, what do you consider acceptable stakeout food?"

"Salted cashews are a must. Caramel Twix. Slim Jims." He snapped his fingers. "And don't forget bottles of Coke or Mountain Dew. Gotta have that extra caffeine, especially when the stakeout has the potential to last all night." He pulled his phone out of his back pocket, checked the screen, and then placed it on the console between them. "What about you?"

Given that he'd just mentioned two of her favorite snacks, she leaned across the console to open the glove compartment and gestured at the contents with a flourish. "Help yourself."

Small bags of peanuts, cashews, and sunflower seeds were arranged inside along with a variety of candy bars, including caramel Twix. She'd just added those this week because putting anything with chocolate in the car before December in Texas was just asking for a melted mess.

"No way." He looked through the choices before giving her a look of approval. "I'm impressed, Durant. Seriously. You're definitely the cop to go on a stakeout with." He reached for a bag of cashews before closing the glove box again.

"Don't get too excited. I don't have a hidden panel full of soda. Unlike you and your kind, I'm not able to utilize an empty bottle when things get desperate. I bring water and drink it sparingly."

"You know, they make a device for women who go camping that allows them to—"

Jenny held up a hand to stop him. "Patterson, I'm not talking about that with you."

The corners of his mouth twitched with a smile he was trying to keep at bay. "I'm just trying to help."

"I don't need your help. As a kid, I grew up in a one-bathroom home with my parents and five siblings. Trust me when I say bathroom time was a commodity that was often bought and traded for." Her siblings liked to tease her, saying she was part camel. It came in handy in instances like this.

She shifted her weight and stretched out her legs. The motion caused an intense ache in her knee that she worked hard to ignore. Once she got home tonight, she'd ice it, and hopefully, it'd be better by tomorrow. Thankfully, Blake didn't seem to notice her discomfort. The last thing she needed was for him to cast doubt on whether she could do her job tomorrow.

Blake tore open the bag of cashews. "I'm not going to lie. I have to admit I'm a bit envious of your family. Don't get me wrong, I'm not sure I could survive with so many siblings around. But to have siblings, or parents, that get along... I hope you know how rare that is."

There were many friends going through school who had dysfunctional families, and it was always hard to watch how that affected them. She was thankful that she hadn't had to experience that herself. "I truly do, and I'm sorry it wasn't like that for you."

He shrugged as though it didn't matter, but she knew differently.

They sat in silence, attention on the Hernandez house, while Blake finished his cashews. After he washed those down with a swig of his soda, he seemed to shake off the melancholy of the previous conversation.

"So, your brother's getting married this weekend. I'll bet your family is excited."

"Oh, yes. Between the siblings, spouses, and kids, we could practically fill up a church before including extended family and friends." Jenny smiled to herself. She was looking forward to seeing all her siblings in one place. "I'm not in the wedding party, and they had the shower last week, so I can just go on Saturday and enjoy."

Although it was fun to be in her sister, Lisa's, wedding as maid of honor two years ago, it was a lot of work, and having no responsibilities other than showing up was a nice change of pace.

"It sounds awesome. And overwhelming." He chuckled. "Are most of your siblings married now?"

She nodded. "After Jared ties the knot, I'll be the last one standing."

A car pulled onto the street and slowly passed several homes, including the Hernandez's, only to turn down another street further up.

Jenny leaned into the back of her seat again and realized that Blake was staring at her. Her cheeks warmed. "What?"

"I find it hard to believe that you're the only one of six siblings who isn't married. Seriously, what's wrong with the men in this town?"

It was a comment he would normally make out of jest, but he didn't look like he was kidding, which made Jenny blush even more.

So, she hadn't found that perfect guy, yet. Truth be told, she was starting to think he didn't exist. And that was okay, because she had a bunch of nieces and nephews to dote on, plus a job that gave her life purpose. The last thing she needed was having to explain her lack of a love life to Blake.

"I'm not talking about that with you, either."

Chapter Six

Obviously, Blake said the wrong thing because Jenny kept conversation centered strictly around the police department, the FBI, and their shared case. Any attempts to swerve into personal territory were quickly blocked with a change in topic.

Every time he thought they were making some kind of headway into becoming friends instead of just partners, she shut him down.

He'd hoped that, after five days of working together, they'd be past this point.

The time dragged all afternoon, and Blake ate way too many snacks. He sent a text to himself with what he'd eaten so he could buy replacements later.

It was fifteen minutes before the end of their shift when a black Toyota Corolla pulled up in front of the Rodriguez home and came to a stop. "We may have something."

"I see it." Jenny leaned forward.

A young man got out of the car and took a quick look around before jogging up the steps to the front door. He couldn't be more than twenty. He pulled a key out of his pocket and let himself in.

Blake glanced at Jenny. "Ms. Rodriguez mentioned that she had four kids. Two younger ones were at home. How old are the other two?"

"That's a good question." Jenny dialed a number on her phone and put it on speaker. Before the call was answered, she told Blake that she was calling the department's resident expert when it came to tracking down information.

"Hey, Logan. I need you to run a search on Marcos Hernandez's sister, Kelly Rodriguez. Can you find out how old her children are?"

"Absolutely. Give me just...a...second." Clacking in the background told them he was busy on the computer. "All right. Kelly Rodriguez has four children. She has two with the husband from her first marriage. Looks like a Samuel is nineteen, and Juanita is sixteen. Then she has two younger boys, ages five and four."

The guy who'd just gone into the house could easily be Samuel Rodriguez. "Does Samuel have a residence listed other than his mother's home?" Blake asked.

"Ding, ding, ding. Point to the FBI agent. Samuel is renting an apartment several streets over." Logan gave them the address. "Anything else you need?"

"That should do it. Thanks, Logan." Jenny ended the phone call. "Are you thinking what I'm thinking?"

"If Marco was as close to these kids as Ms. Rodriguez implied, then he may be staying with his nephew."

"Exactly. I'll call Smith and let her know. See if she wants us to stick around or follow him back to his place."

Officer Smith seemed to think it was a great lead and thanked them both for their part in obtaining it. She only needed them to stick around long enough for another pair of officers to come and take up watch. During that time, the black Corolla never left Kelly's house.

Jenny drove them back to the precinct and parked her car in the gated lot. They walked back to the building together, and there was no mistaking the way she favored her injured knee.

Blake waited for her out front and then walked with her to the main parking lot where they'd both left their personal vehicles. Had that really just been this morning? It truly felt like days.

She finally slowed as they neared her car. "Have a good, uneventful evening."

"Yeah. You, too." She started to turn away when he spoke up to stop her. "How's the ear? Has your hearing returned to normal?"

She reached up and fingered the bandage with a shrug. "Pretty much. Still slightly muted, but since there's no pain, I should be good." A pause. "Thanks for asking. How about you? You okay?"

"Nothing a hot shower and some ibuprofen can't fix. I say that now, though. I'm sure we'll both be feeling it tomorrow."

Jenny chuckled. "Yeah, we will." She shifted her weight from one foot to the other and winced when her right knee seemed to catch. She blew out a frustrated sigh.

"Have you taken a look at it lately?"

"Not since we got back from the courthouse. It'll be fine."

Blake hoped she was right. He stepped forward and cupped her elbow with one hand. "Come on, have a seat. Let's make sure you don't need to go in and have it looked at."

She shook her head, an annoyed expression on her face. "I'm fine, Blake."

"And when I see that for myself, I can verify that with the chief. If you come into work limping like that tomorrow, you're going to get benched."

He waited for the stubborn woman to realize he was right.

With a sigh, she unlocked her car door and eased herself into the driver's seat with a groan. "Remind me not to get so close to an explosion for a while."

He laughed. "The next time you get tempted, just send me a text and I'll talk you out of it."

"Deal."

Jenny carefully pulled up the leg of her pants until her knee was visible. An ugly black bruise had already formed over the kneecap and extended off to one side.

"Durant, you are one tough lady. That looks painful." Without asking permission, he knelt in front of her and gently felt around the joint. "There's not much swelling, so that's a good sign." The skin wasn't overly warm, either. It was silky smooth, though, and that's when Blake realized that he'd lingered longer than he intended.

With a rough clearing of his throat, he pushed back to his feet. "I think you're right. It's just some bruising where you landed on it."

"I'm glad you agree." She hastily rolled the pants leg back down to cover the bruise and avoided eye contact. "I'll go home and ice it for a while."

"Take some ibuprofen."

"Oh, that goes without saying." She finally looked up at him. "Thanks, Blake."

"You're welcome." He ought to turn and go to his truck,

but he wasn't quite ready to say goodbye yet. "Hey, I don't know about you, but I'm starving."

Her right brow rose. "Even after eating half of my snacks?"

"I thought maybe I could buy you dinner. You know, start paying you back for eating so much of your stash. Just two partners who are exhausted after nearly getting blown up and don't want to put much effort into fixing something to eat."

She didn't immediately reject the idea, which was more than he expected.

"I don't know. My knee really is killing me. I'd like to get home, out of these shoes, and put some ice on it."

"Then why don't I pick us up a couple of pizzas and bring them by your place? If you get home and are too tired for company, I'll drop your pizza off and be on my way. Come on, Durant. What do you say?"

He could picture her making a pros and cons list in her head.

Finally, she gave him a short nod. "That sounds like a plan. I'll text you my address. And Patterson? I like supreme pizza on a hand-tossed crust."

Blake chuckled and gave her a salute. "Yes, ma'am." He waited for her address to come through. "I'll see you in a while. Go take care of that knee."

As he drove to a nearby pizza restaurant, placed their order, and waited for their pizzas to bake, he went back over all three cases.

The Destiny Police Department had to be stretched thin trying to figure out who was responsible for the bombing. As much as he wanted to believe it was a random act of violence or a one-time event, he had a bad feeling that wasn't the case.

Chapter Seven

Jenny was glad she normally kept her house picked up. Her parents were known for dropping by unannounced, and it was easier to keep up with the chores than to rush around cleaning like a mad woman. She sat on the couch and glanced around her cozy living room. Her house was small—around twelve hundred square feet—but it was open and well-lit. The couch and a single chair filled the living room space along with a coffee table that looked like a wooden chest and an end table. The minute she saw the coffee table in an antique store, she had to have it.

On the other side of the living room, an arched doorway led to the kitchen and her small dining table. Then, there was a hallway that led to two bedrooms and a bathroom.

Thanks to all the windows and light, Jenny was able to keep a lot of houseplants. She had one sitting just about anywhere that had a space big enough to set a pot on.

She heard the doorbell at the same time that her phone rang. Officer Mari Smith's name came up on caller ID.

"This is Durant." She stood and limped to the door,

checking to make sure it was Blake before opening it and ushering him inside. She pointed to the phone she had pressed against her left ear.

He nodded once and carried two pizza boxes to the bar that separated the living room from the kitchen.

"I wanted to call with a quick update."

"That's great. Agent Patterson is here. I'm going to put you on speaker."

Jenny made her way back to the couch where she'd been resting moments ago. Blake spotted the ice pack she'd dropped onto the coffee table and handed it to her before sitting down on the chair.

Officer Smith's voice came over the speaker. "Good evening, Agent Patterson. Thanks to the two of you, we were able to apprehend Marcos Hernandez at his nephew's place minutes ago. As you guys suspected, the nephew had wanted to prevent his uncle from being arrested again, and it seems that Kelly Rodriguez knew of the arrangement."

That didn't surprise Jenny at all. "I'm surprised Marcos didn't try to skip town."

Blake leaned forward and rested his elbows on his knees. "Was there any evidence that Marcos or members of his family might have been connected to the bombing?"

"Not yet. Logan is going to go through the nephew's laptop. He'll also do a run-through of his financials to see if there's anything unusual there. But my first impression of both Marcos and his nephew is that Marcos simply took advantage of the situation and hoped he could get away with it."

Jenny was thankful that at least one of the cases today had been resolved. "Have you heard from Paris or Walker yet?" Paris was still looking into any connections between the bombing and the defendant who had been killed. If Ms.

Grassle had been the true target, then it was Walker who was trying to piece together who might have been behind it.

"Investigations are ongoing, but nothing is leading us any closer to the bomber. I'd better go. I've got a mountain of paperwork waiting for me before I can head home. Thanks again. You both get some rest tonight."

"Will do. You, too, Mari. Good night."

The call ended, and Jenny shifted her leg so the ice pack covered her knee better. The chill went straight to her bones and made her shiver. She reached for the crocheted blanket on the back of the couch and spread it over her lap.

"I'd feel a whole lot better if we had the bomber in custody tonight."

Blake got to his feet. "You and me both. Rest your knee. If you'll tell me where the plates are, I can bring everything in here."

That sounded good to her. Getting up and down seemed to be what annoyed her knee the most.

"They're in the first upper cabinet on the right."

Minutes later, Blake placed the pizza boxes on the coffee table with two cans of soda, and then handed a plate to Jenny. He opened a box and held it out to her. "Supreme pizza with hand-tossed crust as requested."

Jenny hummed her approval as she moved two large slices over to her plate. Cheese strings hung from the sides until she scooped them onto the pizza with one finger. "I didn't realize how hungry I was until you brought this in. It smells amazing. Thank you."

She took in a deep breath, followed by a large bite. It was the perfect combination of cheese, sauce, and toppings. Most pizza places skimped on the black olives, but not Rocco's Pizzeria.

"You're welcome." Blake chuckled. "I'm glad I ordered

us each a pizza instead of one half-and-half. There might not have been anything left for me."

She wadded up a napkin and threw it at him.

That had him laughing harder. "I'm kidding." He tipped his plate to show three slices of pepperoni. "And you'd better believe I'm getting seconds."

He reclaimed the chair and took a large bite of pizza. When he swallowed, he pointed to the crust. "For the record, hand-tossed is my favorite, too."

They ate in comfortable silence. As Jenny's stomach filled and the ache in her knee eased, she finally found herself relaxing after the craziness of the day. Originally, when she thought about Blake coming over for dinner, she'd been hesitant. Mostly because she was tired and ready for some quiet, but it was also because she didn't have enough energy to combat his teasing and obnoxious comments.

Now, she was glad she wasn't in the house alone. She prayed the courthouse would get all the cases set up again soon. She'd be lying if she said she wasn't nervous about escorting Grassle to her next court appearance. By then, hopefully, they'd have figured out who was behind the bombing.

Blake finished off a slice of pizza and took a drink of soda. "Wouldn't it have made more sense for the bomber to plant the bomb in the actual courtroom where Grassle was going to testify?"

Apparently, she wasn't the only one who was thinking about the case.

"Yes, it would have. Theoretically, they could've taken out the crooked judge right along with her." Not that any of this was okay. But clearly this person didn't care about the lives of others, and if that was the case, it seemed like it would make more sense to take out as many players as possible.

"Maybe they didn't know which courtroom that case was going to be tried in." He picked up another slice of pizza. "So they gambled. When they didn't guess the right courtroom—which they would've realized after seeing the judge enter it earlier in the day—then they didn't have much of a choice."

"They had to detonate when Grassle passed by, hoping that the blast would be enough to kill her." Jenny popped the last bite of buttery-garlic crust into her mouth.

"It makes sense. Again, assuming that it wasn't a random act of violence or a gang execution."

She nodded as she slid her plate onto the coffee table. "With a random act of violence, a person or organization usually steps forward to claim responsibility. If a rival gang was behind it, we might never know, but it's not a typical method they would use. I don't know. Grassle being the target makes the most sense."

"Agreed. It'll be interesting to see what the lab can come up with after going through the bomb debris." Blake ate the last of his crust and looked at the pizza box. "We'll have to check in with the officers tomorrow before heading over to the hotel. Meet there thirty minutes earlier in the morning?"

"Sounds good."

The doorbell rang. Blake looked from her to the door. "Do you want me to get that?"

It was almost definitely her mom. Jenny had assured her parents that she was all right after everything that happened at the courthouse. Knowing Mom, she wanted to see for herself.

The problem was that Blake was here. Mom was likely

to read all kinds of wrong things into that fact. But would it make a difference if she answered the door or he did? Unlikely. Jenny may as well rest her knee.

"Thank you. If it's a shorter woman with a bob haircut, that'll be my mom. Don't say I didn't warn you."

Blake set his plate down on the coffee table and stood, an amused look on his face. "Now you're scaring me."

He looked through the peephole in the door and opened it wide so Jenny could see the person on the front porch.

"Hey, Mom. Come on in."

Mom, who barely hit five foot two, looked up and up at Blake before entering the house. She quirked a hopeful eyebrow. "I didn't realize you had company."

Blake closed and locked the front door before rejoining them in the living room.

"This is Samantha Durant. Mom, meet Blake Patterson. He's with the FBI. We've been assigned to work a case together. He was kind enough to bring pizza by so I didn't have to be on my feet any more than necessary." Jenny lifted the crochet blanket enough for her mom to see the ice on her knee.

"You didn't tell us you'd been hurt. Have you seen a doctor?" Mom sat beside her on the couch. She lightly touched Jenny's knee and then her ear, where she still had a bandage.

"I'm fine. I landed hard—it's just a bruise. But nothing some ice and a little sleep won't fix."

"I'm just thankful you're okay. Both of you." Mom turned her attention to Blake. "Do you live in Destiny?"

Blake reclaimed his seat. "No, ma'am. I'm basically on loan temporarily. I live in Austin."

"That's a shame. How long are you going to be in town?"

Dread washed over Jenny. "Mom? Do you want some pizza? There's plenty." If she could get her mom to start eating, then maybe she wouldn't say what Jenny was afraid she was going to say.

Mom waved her away. "I've got dinner going in the Crock-Pot at the house. Chicken fajitas. You know how much your dad likes those."

So did Jenny—it was one of her favorite meals. Unfortunately, her attempt to change the topic was less than successful.

Mom leaned forward as though she were conspiring with Blake instead of speaking right in front of her daughter.

"Jenny doesn't have a plus one for her brother's wedding this weekend. Now that her friend, Nate, is engaged, she doesn't have anyone else to ask."

Oh, for crying out loud.

Jenny had a feeling her face was the same color as the pizza sauce. "No, Mom. I'm choosing not to ask anyone to go with me. I don't think it's necessary. There will be plenty of people to visit with. Maybe I'll just sit at the kids' table." Hanging out with her nieces and nephews would probably be more fun anyway.

"Nonsense." She waved at Jenny without even looking at her. "Will you be here over the weekend, Blake?"

"I honestly don't know, ma'am. It depends on how long our assignment lasts. I may be heading home before then."

Mom looked so disappointed; you'd think she'd just been told there was a death in the family. "Well, if that changes and you end up in town, I hope you'll come along. You're always welcome. No RSVP needed."

"I appreciate that." Blake picked up his soda, but he couldn't hide his smile behind the can fast enough.

Jenny nearly laughed out loud. She covered her mouth with a paper towel and coughed as Mom finally turned her attention back to her daughter.

"Sweetie, if that knee doesn't heal up, you get to a doctor. If you need any help, promise me you'll let your dad and me know. Okay?" She patted Jenny's knee. "I'd best get back before the fajitas get mushy. I'll see you on Saturday."

With that, like a mini tornado, Mom was gone.

Blake's nearly out-of-control grin morphed into laughter.

"Don't even, or I swear I'll throw this pizza at you." Jenny gave him a stern look, one she hoped he took seriously. Instead, his laughter only intensified. She held out briefly before she was laughing with him.

Minutes later, Jenny swiped at the tears. "I apologize on my mom's behalf. She has like zero boundaries."

"I mean, if I'm still around on Saturday and you need a date..."

"Not on your life."

Chapter Eight

B lake had been in two different car accidents in the past, and neither of them resulted in this many sore muscles. He'd resorted to walking outside for a half hour and then taking a hot shower to get the muscles warmed up.

His thoughts immediately went to Jenny. She'd taken a much harder hit during the explosion. He imagined she was in a great deal of pain this morning. He said a prayer for her and grabbed a quick continental breakfast in the hotel dining area before heading to the precinct. Just like every other morning of this assignment, he'd meet up with Jenny there. Once they checked in with Detectives Walker and Paris, they'd ride over to the hotel where Ms. Grassle was staying.

Blake caught sight of Jenny as soon as he arrived and waited for her at the door. She'd pulled her long, dark hair back into a tight ponytail. As had become the norm with this assignment, she'd dressed casually. Today, she'd chosen a pair of stone-washed jeans and a long-sleeved, maroon blouse. She carried a jacket over one arm.

He greeted her with a smile. "Good morning. Did you get any sleep last night?"

"Actually, I did. It was the waking up and moving part that hurt." She cut him a glance. "In the future, I'll have to make sure I'm better at coordinating my explosions and vacation time." He opened the door, and she entered ahead of him. "How about you?"

"I slept okay." It'd taken a while to fall asleep, and then he had two dreams about the explosion. In one, Jenny was killed. In another, she disappeared. Both times, he woke up in a rush of confusion and panic. "I'm pretty sore myself, though I know it's likely nothing compared to how you feel. You know what they say, right? The third day's the worst."

"I can hardly wait." Her words were thick with sarcasm. To her credit, she wasn't even limping. The only visible evidence of her injuries were the scratches on the backs of her hands and the bandage on her ear.

They entered the bullpen, which seemed only slightly less busy than it had when they'd left yesterday. Detective Paris wasn't in yet, but they found Detective Walker in his office. He waved them in with a smile. "Good to see you both." He turned to Jenny. "Are you feeling okay today?"

"I'm good. Thanks, Nate. We're going to be heading out shortly, but wanted to check in with you first to see if there were any updates." She took a seat, and Blake followed suit.

Walker reclaimed his own chair. "I haven't spoken with Paris yet, but last I heard, there was no evidence pointing to a rival gang being responsible for the bombing. He had a couple of people he planned to interview today along with an informant he wanted to talk to."

Blake hoped Detective Paris's interviews would reveal more information, but he had a feeling that the bombing had nothing to do with gang activity. "What about the bomb itself?"

The detective pulled something up on his computer screen. "A remote was used to set off the bomb, although the whole thing was rather basic. It was nothing that couldn't have been built with directions found on the internet, unfortunately. Of course, any fingerprints that might have remained on the parts used to build it were incinerated in the blast. There was no obvious signature, at least nothing that matched other devices in the system."

Blake was certainly hoping for more detailed results from the lab. "Then we're looking at an amateur bomb-maker. Someone who may have learned how to make one specifically for this situation."

"With the information we currently have, it does seem that way. Which means one of two things is likely to happen if their intended target didn't die in the blast. Either they are new at bomb-making and decide to set aside that form of attack since their first attempt was unsuccessful..."

"...or they seek to perfect their newly-acquired hobby," Jenny finished with a scowl. "I don't particularly care for either option."

Blake didn't like that idea, either. "Jenny and I were talking last night, and Grassle being the target makes the most sense."

Together, he and Jenny walked through their reasoning.

Walker nodded. "I agree with you. Today, I'll be speaking with some of the individuals involved in the original jury tampering case. The two of you question Grassle. See if anyone has been in contact with her. Maybe she'll have more information to share—details she's kept to herself—now that she's had a close brush with death. If a name does come up, let me know, and I'll add them to my list of people to interview."

"That sounds like a plan." Jenny looked at her watch and pushed against the arms of her chair to stand. "Speaking of Grassle, we'd better head that way. We'll check in again later."

"You two stay safe."

"Will do."

Blake walked with Jenny through the building and out to her personal vehicle.

He glanced at Jenny. Now that they were outside, her maroon blouse brought out the rich shades of mahogany in her hair and the chocolate-brown of her eyes. She truly was the most beautiful woman he'd ever met. It took some effort to only glance at her profile as they made their way to the hotel in downtown Destiny.

Instead, he forced his attention to the Christmas decorations the town had put up in their main shopping areas. Red ribbons were wrapped around the poles, sparkling red baubles hung from eaves and signs, and a large tree was decorated from top to bottom with lights and ornaments.

"Wow, Destiny goes all out for the holidays, doesn't it?"

Jenny chuckled. "Yes, it does. There's usually some kind of Christmas-related activity every weekend, too. Pancakes with Santa, carols and cocoa, holiday extravaganza. Our local chamber of commerce does everything it can to get citizens to shop locally."

"That helps to build a sense of community, too." There was a lot to be said for smaller towns. Although in larger cities, some neighborhoods adopted a similar approach to accentuate their small-town charm. "Are your brother and his future bride incorporating the holiday into their wedding?"

"No, not really." She stopped at a red light and glanced over at him. "They chose Felicity Grove for their venue. The place is gorgeous during the spring months if you want an outdoor wedding. But they also have this rustic building with a vaulted ceiling and plenty of room for both the wedding and the reception, although they're hoping the weather will hold out to be able to use the large, covered patio for the reception."

The light flashed green again, and she turned onto the block where the hotel was located. Once they got there and up to Grassle's room on the second floor, any personal discussions would be put on hold. That was why Blake enjoyed the drive in so much.

"It does sound beautiful. Now, is this the brother who lives in Destiny?"

"Yes. Personally, I would've chosen the same venue, but I would've waited until spring. They have some gorgeous areas there where the trees create canopies overhead, and lights hang from the branches. It's almost magical."

There was a wistful tone to her voice, and she must've realized it because she blushed furiously and became incredibly intent on her search for a parking place.

Blake pretended not to notice so he wouldn't embarrass her further. "So, how likely do you think it is that Grassle is going to cooperate with our line of questioning this morning?"

"Oh, she'll be about as cooperative as a cat during bath time."

He chuckled at the comparison, but it wasn't inaccurate. Grassle was either aloof or hissing with claws out. "So, do you want to play good cop or bad cop?"

That had Jenny smiling. "Something tells me she won't differentiate between the two."

Chapter Nine

Once they reached Annie Grassle's hotel room just after eight in the morning, Blake and Jenny checked in with the night shift for an update on how things stood. Apparently, Ms. Grassle had turned in after ten the night before, and they didn't hear a peep from her after that.

The other officers left, and they closed and secured the door.

Blake took in the multiple tiny glass bottles that were sitting on the coffee table and on top of the mini -fridge. No wonder the night shift hadn't seen Grassle since she went to bed. It looked like they were about to find out what a hungover witness was like.

Jenny shot him a foreboding look. Apparently, they were on the same wavelength.

They set their belongings in a spot next to the small couch. Both had backpacks that held snacks, a packed lunch, chargers for their phones, extra ammo for their weapons, and a bulletproof vest. They didn't need to wear them all the time in the hotel, but if there was an emergency or they needed to escort Grassle somewhere else, putting the vests on would be one of their highest priorities.

They both kept earpieces in and tuned to a channel that would be used to communicate with them if needed. In order to transmit, they needed to activate the microphone by tapping on the earpiece. It was just as easily deactivated. That way, general conversation throughout the day didn't clog the channel. And there was potential for the day to be a long one.

Blake hoped to have the opportunity to talk to Jenny about her mom and the wedding this weekend. But while they were on duty, there were no personal discussions. He took his job seriously and would remain one hundred percent professional.

He allowed a ghost of a smile as he thought about the interaction between Jenny and her mom. He imagined them driving each other crazy sometimes, and yet, it was clear there was a deep love and affection there. No doubt Mama Durant would do anything to protect her daughter.

And, apparently, she had no qualms about trying to set her up with Blake—a man she didn't know from Adam.

He suppressed a chuckle. Truthfully, he'd enjoy going to the wedding with Jenny. For one thing, watching her interact with her large family would be interesting. Most of all, though, he'd appreciate the opportunity to spend time with her where they'd feel free to talk about their interests and opinions—the kinds of personal topics that were left off the table while on the job.

Not for the first time, he wished he lived closer to Destiny.

Grassle didn't roll out of bed until nearly noon. When she emerged from the bedroom, she shot them an annoyed look, flinched against the bright lights, and then groaned. "I wasn't sure whether you guys would be back after someone tried to kill me."

"We don't know for certain that you were the target." Jenny's voice was even.

Grassle didn't look convinced. She pressed a hand to her head and squeezed her eyes closed. "I need some coffee."

Jenny had put on a pot earlier. Blake, feeling sorry for the witness, filled a paper cup with the black liquid and handed it over.

No thanks were offered as she grasped the cup with both hands and breathed in the aroma.

Grassle sat at the little wooden table and nursed her coffee. Eventually, she reached for one of the pastries that had been brought up for her earlier that morning. "You guys any closer to figuring out who set the bomb?"

Jenny carefully lowered herself onto the couch. "Not yet. Trust me, though, some of our best people are working on it."

He'd noticed she took some medication just a little while ago. Hopefully, it helped ease her aches.

"I just hope they get the hearing rescheduled soon. I want to get this over with."

"As soon as we get the word, we'll let you know," he promised.

Even though the woman drove him crazy, and she was far from pleasant, he could certainly sympathize with how her whole life had changed overnight. Sure, her own decisions had led to that. But still, it wouldn't be easy. Did she have family she was leaving behind? Friends?

"See that you do."

And with that, the sympathy evaporated.

He exchanged a look with Jenny, who just subtly shook her head. She looked down at her cell phone and typed something out. A minute later, his own pinged. He glanced at the screen.

We're seeing her at her worst during less-than-ideal circumstances.

She wasn't wrong.

There had been plenty of difficult times in his life when he was grateful someone else extended a level of grace that he didn't deserve. In the end, that kindness helped him through.

It cost very little to do the same for Annie Grassle right now.

They allowed her to finish her first cup of coffee before starting to question her.

Jenny began the interview. "Ms. Grassle, have you been in contact with anyone over the last five days? This could be through phone, text, e-mail, or even in passing at some point."

Grassle tipped the cup to her lips, then set it down on the table harder than necessary when no coffee came out.

Blake got the coffee pot from the dinette and poured her another cup. As usual, she didn't even give him a nod of thanks.

She stared at the black liquid as though she expected it to answer for her.

"Ms. Grassle?" Jenny's tone was calm. Encouraging.

The fact she could accomplish that when Blake knew how frustrated she was probably feeling was a testament to her training and strength.

"I was encouraged by my lawyer as well as law enforcement not to contact anyone until after the trial was over, and even then, I may not have the opportunity." She swallowed hard and took a sip of the coffee that had to have burned her tongue.

Blake decided to try rewording the question. "Has anyone attempted to contact *you* in the last five days? Have you received any more threats, or has anyone asked you to give them something in exchange for your freedom once the trial is over?"

Grassle seemed to hesitate as she set her coffee cup on the table. "There have been no new threats."

Jenny's eyes narrowed as she leaned forward. "But you have been in contact with someone."

Their witness only shrugged.

He could demand that she tell them who it was, but that would get them nowhere. Instead, he recalled some of the statistics he'd read about WITSEC.

"Look, Ms. Grassle. The fact is, WITSEC has a one hundred percent success rate for those witnesses who follow the rules and guidelines. They are there for a reason and will keep you safe. Is it easy to leave everyone and everything behind? Of course not. I can only imagine how difficult this must be for you."

He moved to sit in the chair across the table from her. "Once you've been assigned your new identity and have been relocated, we can't prevent you from reaching out to someone from your old life. But every time you open a line of communication, you not only risk the chance of someone discovering your new location, but there's a possibility potential enemies will try to use that person against you."

For the first time since they'd met her, Grassle's eyes teared up. She propped her elbows on the table and cradled her head in her hands with a heavy sigh. "I wish this could be like it is in the movies, where everyone associated with this nightmare goes to jail so I can go back to my normal life."

Jenny retrieved a box of tissues from the bathroom and set them on the table in front of Grassle.

"Is there anyone that you're particularly worried about? Someone that might be harassed or even targeted by the people behind this whole mess?"

"My sister. Rebecca Mills. I mean, she had nothing to do with any of this, but she's the person I'm closest to. I wish she would go into the witness protection program with me." Grassle swallowed hard and pressed her tissue to her nose. "But she's got a husband. Kids."

Jenny glanced at Blake before she asked her next question. "Annie, did you have anything to do with the bombing?"

Grassle lowered the tissue and looked at Jenny in shock. "No!" She blew her nose again and crumpled the tissue in her hand. "I know I made some poor decisions. I wish I could say I had some great reason for accepting the bribe, but I don't expect that it would've been nice not to worry about money for a change. But I would *never* hurt someone, and I would *never* want someone to hurt others on my behalf."

She spoke with such conviction that Blake was inclined to believe her. Especially in combination with her look of shock when Jenny had asked her about the bomb in the first place.

Blake got the small trash can by the door and brought it over. Grassle threw her used tissue away and plucked out a clean one.

He sat down again. "I believe you. Do you know anyone involved in the case that might not feel the same way? Someone you can see being fine with hurting other people?"

"I honestly don't know." She swiped at the corners of her eyes. "Everything was done so secretively. I didn't even know the judge was involved until well after the fact. I didn't know my contact beforehand, either."

Jenny poured coffee into a paper cup and took a sip. "Think back to the courthouse yesterday. Was there anyone there that you recognized? It could've been in the hallway or after the explosion during all the panic. Did anyone seem familiar to you?"

To Grassle's credit, she closed her eyes and seemed to truly focus on the question. After several moments, she shook her head. "No. I didn't recognize anyone." She looked from Jenny to Blake. "Do you think whoever set off the bomb might try to kill me again?"

Blake leaned forward. "If you were the target at the courthouse—and we still haven't definitively established you were—then yes, there's a strong possibility they might try to come after you again. But our job is to keep you safe."

Chapter Ten

After their conversation with Grassle, Jenny called Nate to update him on what they found out—or rather, what they didn't. But she did pass along Grassle's sister's name. She couldn't imagine a scenario where Rebecca would be involved in the bombing.

Nate agreed but said he'd probably swing by and make sure that Rebecca and her family were doing okay and that no one had been threatening them or asking about Grassle.

Jenny didn't know Grassle very well, but she had a feeling that following all WITSEC's rules was going to be difficult for her. If there was someone Jenny thought would reach out to a family member after she was relocated, it was Annie Grassle.

"Oh," Nate began, "I did talk to security at the courthouse. Many people had access to the building before it officially opened for court proceedings. Janitors cleaned everything from top to bottom, and that included making sure the trash was emptied. Maintenance was on hand to change out light bulbs, make sure TVs were plugged in and ready, and fix anything that needed it. No one noticed anything unusual in that courtroom where the explosion took place. One of the janitors remembered it specifically because he'd had to switch out a trash receptacle completely since the old one was cracked. There was no device."

"So we're looking at a five-ish hour window between the janitor switching out the receptacle and the explosion."

"Logan's going over security footage, but so far, he's got nothing. That trash can was in one of many blind spots, so we didn't have a camera on it at all," Nate explained. "That and the bomb was relatively small. It could've entered the courthouse hidden in a briefcase or set outside a window for someone to open and bring in. Metal detectors only work if the weapon or device passes through it."

"Very true."

By the time she ended her call with Nate, their witness had excused herself to take a shower and get dressed, leaving Jenny and Blake in the living room alone again.

Jenny retrieved her lukewarm cup of coffee from the little table and sat down on the couch. "Nate's going to check into the sister." She told him about Nate's investigation into the courthouse and who might have had access to the room before everyone else arrived.

Blake frowned. "We may never know how the bomb got there."

They steered the conversation to the weather and news before falling silent while they each checked their phones for messages and e-mails to help pass the time until Grassle returned.

Once she did, they got her lunch order and called down to room service. When it arrived, Blake left the room to retrieve the meal and bring it in himself.

While Grassle ate her hot lunch, Jenny retrieved her

lunch box from her backpack and laughed when she saw that Blake, too, had brought cold leftover pizza.

He lifted a slice and tapped it to hers. "Cheers."

They were nearly done with lunch when their earpieces crackled to life.

"This is Walker. We may have a situation near your location. Be alert."

She activated her microphone and responded. "Received. Standing by."

Blake abandoned the rest of his pizza and got to his feet. He picked up Jenny's backpack and tossed it to her before reaching into his own to retrieve his bullet-proof vest along with a spare that they had for the witness if it was ever needed.

Grassle set her fork down and pushed away from the table. "What's going on?"

"We're just being cautious," Jenny assured her as she helped her put on the vest.

The poor woman didn't look convinced.

Suddenly, the fire alarm went off, filling the room with a loud, piercing tone. The light on one wall flashed persistently.

Jenny finished putting on her vest and spoke into her radio. "This is Durant. What's going on?"

Ms. Grassle got to her feet, both her hangover and lunch forgotten.

Jenny's earpiece crackled, and she knew Blake's had as well. "Someone called the hotel lobby with a bomb threat. One of the employees immediately pulled the fire alarm to get people to evacuate the building. Stand by."

Blake moved to stand near Grassle. "There's been a bomb threat. We may have to evacuate the hotel. Grab anything you want to take with you and stay in the bedroom until one of us comes to get you."

Grassle nodded, her eyes wide with fear, and she hurried from the room.

Blake tapped his earpiece. "Has anyone been able to verify that a bomb is present?"

"Not at this time."

Blake frowned.

They couldn't risk keeping the witness in place if the bomb threat was legit. Jenny sure didn't like the idea of moving her, either, though. She exchanged a glance with Blake, confirming that he was following the same train of thought.

Nate's voice sounded in Jenny's ear. "An unaccompanied bag has been spotted in the dining room. Bomb squad is five minutes out. Evacuate the witness using plan B. Another team will be in place and waiting."

"Understood."

They'd mapped and discussed all possible evacuation routes in preparation for this assignment, along with their risks. In this case, they would be going out the window and using the fire escape to get from the second floor to the alley below.

It wasn't an ideal means of escape, and it left their witness vulnerable while they climbed down. Compared to a potential bomb, though, it seemed like the least risky option.

Jenny found Grassle in the bedroom, a small backpack slung over one shoulder and her hands clasped together.

Jenny motioned her to follow. "We're going to have to go out the fire escape. Come on."

She knew Blake wasn't a big fan of this plan. Not that the alternative was any better. If there was a bomb, and the person who planted it was watching, they might cause it to detonate the moment they tried to vacate to the ground floor from within the hotel.

At the same time, the idea of Grassle being visible for as long as two minutes while climbing down the ladder didn't set well, either.

Jenny prayed that, if there really was a bomb, everyone could get out of the building safely.

They got back to the main room where Blake had opened the window and lowered the ladder.

Jenny turned to address Grassle. "I'm going to go first, and then you come right after me. You and I are going to descend the ladder with you right above me so that I can shield you as we go. Agent Patterson will follow us. Keep your head low and stay focused. Do you understand?"

Grassle nodded, her eyes darting to the window.

"Let's go." Blake waved them forward as he scanned the alley and nearby buildings.

With hands gripping the railing on either side of Grassle, Jenny tried to shield her as much as possible. She shoved thoughts of another bomb out of her mind and made her way down the fire escape ladder as quickly as she could. She glanced up to see that Blake was following just above their witness. Two officers were waiting near the base of the ladder to help whisk Grassle to safety as soon as they reached the ground.

A popping noise pierced the air. Jenny pressed her body close to Grassle's to pen her in. "Keep your head down."

She barely got the words out before two more shots echoed between the buildings. A white-hot pain erupted in her right side, forcing the air from her lungs. She tried to keep her grip on the rails, but her fingers automatically relaxed, and she started to fall.

Chapter Eleven

Everything seemed to move in slow motion as Jenny fell the remaining eight feet to land in the alley below. Her back hit first, immediately followed by her head. She registered Grassle's scream as the other woman scrambled down the ladder. People shouted around her, and officers escorted Grassle away from the building.

Blake jumped from the ladder and landed beside Jenny, his expression a mix of determination and worry.

She wanted to tell him that she would be okay. She tried to gasp for air, but it was as though her body had forgotten how to breathe. Her chest tightened, and panic began to creep in.

He pulled her to her feet and all but dragged her around the unmarked police car. She collapsed to her knees behind it. Air finally forced its way into her lungs, and she gulped, her head pounding.

Sounds overlapped as officers called out updates, directions were given, and sirens sounded in the distance.

Jenny focused on herself and the pain radiating from the side Blake was examining. He gave her bulletproof vest a pat and leaned back against the car with a murmured, "The shot hit your vest. Thank God."

"Amen," she croaked out. "Grassle?"

"Safe, thanks to you." He raised his voice. "Where are we with the shooter?"

Officer Josh Carrington knelt beside them and gave Jenny an assessing once over. "In the wind. The shots came from a window in the office building behind us. Officers are searching the building for the shooter. Bomb squad is checking out the backpack in the hotel now. We should have some answers soon."

"And an ambulance?" The question came from Blake.

Jenny wanted to insist that she didn't need one, but man, breathing in deep was uncomfortable, and her head was throbbing. If roles were reversed and Blake had taken the hit to his vest, she'd insist on the same thing.

"On the way." Carrington stood again and moved to get a better view of the street.

She sent up a silent prayer for the safety of the bomb squad as well as the officers chasing down the shooter.

Blake put a hand on her shoulder to steady her. "The bomb threat was intended to flush us out."

Jenny nodded. "They knew where we were keeping Grassle and waited for us to evacuate the building." She winced as she shifted her weight and sat down on the pavement.

"Hopefully, that means there isn't really a bomb."

At least there would be *some* good news to come out of this mess.

Her vest was tight to the point of making her feel almost claustrophobic. It took a lot of concentration to focus on anything else when she really wanted to rip it off and breathe easier. She prayed the ambulance would arrive soon and that there had been no major damage from the impact of the bullet.

"Jenny?" Blake had leaned in until they were face-to-face. "Are you okay?"

He used one hand to brush hair out of her face and deposited it behind her ear. He lingered for a moment, his thumb resting against the bandage from yesterday. The gentle, caring touch somehow managed to put her more at ease while it caused her heart to race.

Blake dropped his hand. "I'm inclined to ask Chief Dolman to put you in a bubble until all of this gets sorted out."

She knew he was kidding, but she still pierced him with a stern stare. "Not going to happen."

Carrington came back into view. "Ambulance is coming through now. How're you doing?"

"I'm fine." Even though her side still hurt, breathing was slowly becoming easier. Unfortunately, her headache wasn't improving yet.

"Good. There's no sign of the shooter. He or she seems to be long gone. There was also no bomb in the backpack. Bomb squad is going to do a thorough sweep of the hotel to make sure it's clear."

Jenny and Blake exchanged a look. It was just like they thought—the call had been used to make everyone evacuate the building.

The ambulance approached and pulled to a stop on the other side of the car. Blake stood. "Was anyone else hurt?"

"A few scrapes and maybe a sprained wrist when people practically trampled each other to get out of the hotel. Nothing serious, though." Carrington waved over an EMT.

When Jenny saw that it was Curtis, the same EMT

who had treated them after the explosion, she might have laughed if she hadn't been so afraid that it would hurt. She did offer a smile.

"Hey." He knelt on the pavement beside her. "I take it as a good sign when my patient can smile. You took a shot to the vest?"

Blake stepped back to give them more room.

Jenny shifted just enough to turn her right side toward Curtis. "Not sure if the shot knocked the air out of me or if falling did."

Curtis's eyes narrowed. "How far did you fall? Did you hit your head?"

She started to nod, but it hurt too much. "Yes. About eight feet. I landed on my back."

"Okay. Let's get the vest off and take a look."

She steeled herself as, with Curtis's help, she got the bulletproof vest off. Even though she knew that the vest had stopped the bullet, it was still a relief to see that the shirt underneath hadn't been damaged or stained with her blood.

Curtis gently lifted her shirt to just below her chest.

She craned her neck to get a look at her ribs and gasped. A combination of red and purple the size of her palm radiated from a central point of impact. "Well, that's colorful, isn't it?"

Blake chuckled, but when she looked up at him, there was only worry on his face.

"I'm good," she said, her tone firm. Then she looked at Curtis. "Right?"

Curtis said nothing as he carried out his examination, pressing on her ribs and asking her to inhale and exhale at different points. Finally, he gave a satisfactory nod. "You may have two cracked ribs. None of them feel broken, though. You're going to have quite the bruise, and it may take a couple of weeks to heal completely. But you should be okay. Wrapping your ribs will help reduce the pain."

Jenny grasped her pants leg with her left hand and braced herself as Curtis wrapped her ribs. It was a painful process that felt much better when he'd finished.

He took a flashlight out of his pocket and shined it in her eyes. The bright light made her flinch, and the throbbing in her head intensified.

"You may have a concussion. It's likely a minor one, but I'm going to need to take you to the hospital to have it evaluated. They'll want to get an x-ray of those ribs, too."

She groaned. "Great."

"Can you walk to the ambulance, or do you want me to get a stretcher?"

"I can walk."

Blake reached down and offered her a hand. She accepted it, thankful for his help in getting to her feet. Even when she was standing, he continued to cup her elbow as though he were afraid she might fall again. She didn't mind the extra support. It took a lot to stand straight and not stoop against the headache.

With Blake on one side and Curtis on the other, they helped her into the ambulance. She eased onto the stretcher and laid back before closing her eyes against the light that seemed to be making her headache even worse.

Curtis was probably right about the concussion.

Blake's voice came from nearby on her right. "I'm riding along."

That must have been fine because Curtis spoke from the other side. "I'll be right here. Maddy is the one driving up front.

Jenny didn't have the energy to argue. The ambulance began to move, and she kept her eyes closed for the ride.

A few minutes in, Blake rested a hand on her forearm. "You awake?"

"Yep."

"Good. I've got a serious question here," he began, "and I believe it's one that only you and a handful of others could answer." He paused for dramatic effect as he pinned her with a serious look. "Which was more painful? The explosion, or being shot in the vest?"

Curtis chuckled, but it sounded muffled.

Jenny would've rolled her eyes had they been open. The shooter—who was likely also the bomber—was still at large, and Grassle's life was in danger. This wasn't the time for jokes. "Leave it to you to have something ridiculous to say at the most inappropriate time."

"I don't know that now is the *most* inappropriate."

She opened her eyes just enough to see he'd given her one of those grins that probably made women fan themselves. Of course, it had no effect on her. At all.

Right.

She said nothing as they rode the rest of the way to the hospital in silence. Maddy announced that they were pulling up to the ambulance bay.

Blake gave her arm a light squeeze. "You never did answer my question." He hadn't moved his hand once since they'd gotten into the ambulance. "Research, Jenny. It's for research."

"The explosion. Hands down."

Chapter Twelve

Blake kept a hand on Jenny's arm as they pulled into the ambulance bay at the hospital. He knew she was okay, but the steady rise and fall of her chest coupled with the warmth of her skin was reassuring.

He wasn't going to lie: watching her fall from that ladder and not knowing where she'd been shot or how bad it was, had been terrifying. In that moment, one of the biggest regrets of his life was not insisting that he go first to cover Grassle.

The officers below would have visually swept the area for any danger, and Blake had done the same from the hotel window. He wanted to blame himself for not spotting the shooter but knew good and well that the shooter could have stepped up to the window in the office building while they were mid-climb.

He tried to shake off the different scenarios playing through his head. Her vest had stopped the bullet. Bruised ribs were no picnic, and neither was a concussion. But she was alive.

One thing was certain—Jenny was one of the strongest people he'd ever known. He'd admired her since their first assignment together, but working with her for an extended period of time during this last week had only reinforced that.

They made a good team. He wished he had more of a chance to talk to her outside of work. Maybe go on a hike or hang out and watch TV.

Okay, he'd really like to ask her out on a date. Sometimes, he worried that his growing feelings for her were obvious. But if she'd figured it out, she hadn't let on.

Which led Blake to wonder how she would react if she *did* know. The possibility that she might have feelings for him, too, made him want to say something, until he reminded himself that she was far more likely to look at him like he'd grown a third eye and send him on his way.

Maybe after the case was over.

The back of the ambulance opened, and Curtis got out first. He gave a report of Jenny's condition to the individuals waiting in the bay. Blake quickly extended a hand to the EMT. "Thank you."

"Of course. I hope her recovery is quick."

Blake gave a nod and then jogged to catch up with Jenny. "Do you want me to call anyone for you?"

"Definitely not. I don't need my family worrying about me while they're finalizing wedding preparations."

He'd respect that, although after meeting her mom, he had a feeling Jenny would be hearing from them once they found out she'd been hurt. For his part, he might not be able to go back with Jenny, but he was going to be in the waiting room.

They wheeled her into a small room, and he had to wait until they'd cleared the doorway to follow them in. He went to the front of the bed, where he found her looking at him, her dark eyes half-closed.

"Blake? Can you stay?"

The request so surprised him that it took a moment for him to process her words and respond. If there was only one thing he knew about Jenny Durant, it was that she was fiercely independent, and the fact that *she'd* asked *him* to stay with her was not lost on him.

"Of course. I'm not going anywhere."

Jenny nodded and closed her eyes again.

Apart from a few minutes when Blake stepped outside so the nurse could help Jenny into a hospital gown, he never left the room. For the next hour, Blake stayed nearby while a doctor and nurses took care of her. They x-rayed her chest and confirmed she had two cracked ribs before rewrapping them. After that, they did several tests and determined that, while she did have a mild concussion, she didn't need an MRI or CT scan.

"You are going to need to limit your activity for a few days," Doctor Prescott told her.

His gray hair, round face, bristled eyebrows, and kind mannerisms made Blake think of Andy Griffith as Matlock.

"You should be able to return to work in a limited fashion on Monday, provided the headaches have ceased. For the most part, listen to your body, and if what you're doing causes more pain, then you know it's time to slow down."

Jenny was sitting up, an IV in her right arm, and her hair looking much darker than usual against the white of the pillowcase behind her head. "I have a wedding to go to on Saturday. That shouldn't be a problem, right? It's here in town."

The doctor slid a pair of glasses into place and made a

note on his tablet. "It shouldn't be a problem if you take it easy. Get lots of rest, drink plenty of fluids, and avoid driving through the weekend. If you don't feel better by Monday, you should make an appointment and speak with your doctor. I recommend scheduling a follow-up anyway."

"I will. Thank you. Does that mean I can get out of here?"

Blake chuckled, and the doctor laughed out loud.

"I don't see why not. We'll get those discharge papers going." With that, he gave her a kind smile and left the room, followed by the nurse.

Jenny glanced at the IV in her arm. "I hope she comes back soon to take this out. I hate the way IVs feel."

Blake wasn't a fan of them, either. It didn't help that it took the nurse three tries to get the IV into place. He could already see some bruising on her arm from the earlier attempts.

"I'm sure the nurse will be back before long." Even though experience had taught him that it often took next to forever to finally get discharged from an ER visit.

His phone pinged with a text. "Detective Walker says he and the chief are out in the waiting room. If you'll give them your keys, they'll make sure your car is brought over from the hotel. Are you up to visitors?"

Jenny brightened at the idea. "Absolutely. It'd be good to get an update on everything, too."

"I'll send them your room number." He had to lean into the hall to find it.

Moments later, he spotted them and waved them in.

Chief Dolman greeted her with a squeeze to the shoulder while Detective Walker walked around the bed to give her a hug. They insisted on knowing how she was doing, so Jenny gave them the details. "I should be able to return to work on Monday."

Blake didn't miss her wording there, focusing on when she'd be back as opposed to the fact that she'd be unable to work tomorrow.

The chief studied her closely. "You had a close call today. If I remember correctly, you've got quite a bit of vacation time banked. Taking next week off for some rest and relaxation wouldn't be a bad idea."

"I appreciate that, sir, but I'm sure I'll be fine to come back in on Monday."

Blake bit his tongue. After the last two days, he'd be tempted to make that week of vacation mandatory. She was stubborn—a trait of hers that he both respected and found frustrating at the same time.

She motioned to the door. "They should be back with discharge papers soon. How's Grassle?"

"She's safe and unharmed, thanks to you and Agent Patterson." The chief gave each of them a nod of approval. "Well done. I've assigned another detail to protect our witness."

Blake wasn't surprised. Even if Jenny hadn't been hurt, the shooter had been close enough to nearly kill Ms. Grassle and probably saw his and Jenny's faces. A new detail would be a better choice now.

Unfortunately, it also meant that his assignment with Jenny was over.

Jenny nodded her agreement. "I completely understand. Has there been any word on when her testimony will be needed?"

"It looks like it'll be Monday."

"After this last week, it'd be nice to see that case

wrapped up." Jenny subconsciously scratched at the skin around where the IV had been inserted.

Blake stepped forward. "I'd like to stick around through Monday as well, Chief, if you have no objections. It'd be nice to see the case through, even if we aren't on the safety detail."

Chief Dolman gave a decisive nod. "We'd be happy to have your assistance." His phone rang, and he glanced at the screen. "It's my wife. I'd better take this and get back to the station. Walker, if you'll bring them up to speed, please." He pointed at Jenny. "Get some rest. That's an order."

With that, he answered the call as he stepped into the hall. "Hey, Chloe. Sorry I missed your call earlier..."

Walker closed the door behind the chief. When he turned around, his expression had grown serious.

Jenny stopped scratching at her arm. "What is it, Nate?"

Walker moved to sit in one of the two chairs in the room. "The chief and I were going over some of the preliminary information from the shooting. We need to consider the possibility that you were the target today."

Chapter Thirteen

Wait, what? Jenny looked from Nate to Blake. Her partner seemed as surprised by the idea that someone was after her as she did. Considering all the other working theories, this seemed the least likely. "What makes you say that?"

Nate waited for Blake to claim the other chair. "If the shooter had wanted to kill Grassle, it would've made more sense to take her out before she got on the ladder or once she'd reached the ground. Shooting after you started to climb down made it nearly impossible to hit her, especially from the angle the shooter was aiming from."

Blake frowned. "The first two shots missed completely. The third hit Jenny's vest. Once she fell, Grassle was completely exposed."

"Exactly. They didn't take that final shot to kill Grassle."

The guys were talking as if Jenny wasn't sitting right there. As far as she was concerned, there wasn't nearly enough evidence to convince her they were right. "The whole thing was sloppy. Maybe the fact that they hit a police officer instead of their intended target sent them running."

"I agree that it was sloppy." Nate leaned back in his chair until the front two legs lifted off the floor. "The shooter was clearly not an expert marksman, regardless of the target. Thank God for that. We've got officers still going through the scene, but it's clear those first two shots went wide. We're hoping to recover one of those bullets so that ballistics can run it through the system."

Jenny shifted on the bed. Seriously, where was the nurse? "What about the one that hit my vest?"

"There were only fragments left. Looks like a .45."

The room felt suddenly cold as a chill ran down the back of her neck. The idea was far-fetched, but just entertaining the possibility was enough to make her feel even more fortunate to be alive.

"Let's say you're right, and I really was the target. Why now? Why not two weeks ago or last month? Why didn't they take the shot when I walked to my car first thing this morning or stopped to get my mail?" There was no shortage of easier opportunities to kill her if someone had been watching her at all. It wasn't exactly a reassuring thought.

Nate lowered his chair back to all four legs with a thud and held out a hand to stop her. "I'm not dismissing our original theory that Grassle is the target, but I do think this new angle is worth pursuing. I'd rather be cautious and rule it out than ignore it and put you at risk."

As much as Jenny hated the idea, he wasn't wrong. "What are you suggesting we do?"

"You need to lie low. Which you should be doing anyway after your injury." Nate gave her a pointed look. "I know Jared's wedding is on Saturday. We'll arrange for a few officers to be on-site—discretely, of course."

"Then you're not recommending I skip the wedding?"

Nate chuckled. "With *your* family? That would never fly. And we don't have enough evidence to warrant that. But with officers on site and someone there to watch your back," he tilted his head toward Blake, "I think you'll be good to go. Again, this is all just a precaution."

Jenny blinked at Nate. Was he really suggesting that Blake should go to the wedding with her? Nate knew her mother would grab onto the fact she was bringing a plus one like a drowning woman clinging to a life preserver. Jenny would never, ever hear the end of it.

Blake lifted both hands as though he were giving up after some kind of fight. "I'm happy to go to the wedding with you, Jenny. You're not supposed to drive yourself until Monday anyway."

Nate cleared his throat and covered his mouth, but not before a hint of a smile peeked out.

She was about to say the two of them should go together and leave her out of it when the nurse marched back into the room with a bright smile. "Why don't we disconnect that IV and get you out of here?"

Jenny shot them both looks to let them know the conversation wasn't over before turning her attention to the nurse who was already working to pull the IV from her arm. "That would be great, thank you."

Nate stood. "I need to get back to the station. Patterson, we brought Jenny's car and left it in the north parking lot. Can you make sure she gets home okay, please?"

"Of course." Blake stood as well. "I'm going to need to pick up my truck from the station..."

It wasn't easy to keep up with their conversation while

trying to answer the nurse's questions. Finally, the nurse pressed gauze against the spot where the IV was removed and wrapped some tape around her arm to keep it from bleeding.

"There we go. Now, I've got your discharge papers right here. I need your signature." She handed Jenny a clipboard and a pen. "Perfect. Here are your aftercare instructions. Dr. Prescott recommends following up with your general practitioner at some point next week."

With a happy smile, the nurse handed her a bag filled with her clothing. "Do you need help changing?"

Jenny was going to have to change clothes on her own later tonight and tomorrow, so she might as well get used to it now. She shook her head. "I've got it. Thank you."

"Absolutely. We'll get out of your hair so you can get dressed. When you're ready to leave, let someone at the nurse's station know, and we'll take you down to your car."

The men had moved off to talk near the door, and now they stepped into the hallway with the nurse right behind them.

For the first time since she'd arrived at the hospital, she had the room to herself. She dressed as quickly as she could, which wasn't easy between her pounding headache and the pain in her side. Funny how she didn't even notice her knee now.

She looked at her reflection in the mirror and grimaced. No wonder the guys had been looking at her like she might break any minute. She took the elastic band from her hair, releasing her messy ponytail. With her fingertips, she ruffled her hair, so at least it didn't look quite so bad. With deliberate movements, she made her way to the door and opened it.

"You guys can come back in. I just need to gather my stuff."

Both men were in the room again before she'd finished the invitation. Nate gathered the rest of her things and put them in the plastic bag that held her clothes earlier. Meanwhile, Blake folded her discharge papers.

Nate handed the bag over to Blake.

"Jenny, Patterson is going to take you home and hang out there until someone is able to bring his truck by your house later this evening."

She folded her arms and tried her best not to show just how much her head hurt right now. "Is this little arrangement because you're afraid I can't take care of myself? Or because you think I need a bodyguard now?"

"Maybe it's because you have friends who refuse to let you do things on your own." He gave her a gentle hug. "Get some rest. I promise I'll keep you in the loop."

"You better."

He flashed her a reassuring smile and left the room.

She turned her attention to Blake. "Was this his idea or yours?"

"It's one that was mutually agreed upon. Come on, let's get you out of here before the doctor changes his mind."

As much as Jenny would have preferred to walk out of the hospital on her own, she was thankful for the wheelchair. Every little bump sent a throb through her head and made her ribs ache. She'd been given some pain medication in her IV, but it didn't do a whole lot. She hated to admit it, but what she really needed was some sleep.

She'd given her car keys to Blake. By the time the nurse had pushed her wheelchair to the front of the hospital, Blake was already waiting. He got out and helped her ease into the passenger seat.

Thankfully, her place was less than ten minutes away.

Jenny watched as the world went by her window. "Do you really think it's possible I'm the target?" She looked at his profile.

"Honestly? I'm not sure, but we aren't taking any chances."

Chapter Fourteen

After Blake helped Jenny inside, he closed the front door and looked around the cozy living room. A large cage of some kind sat in one corner. It was filled with plants and had a light fixture overhead that lit up the enclosure. How had he not noticed it when he was there before?

"What's in the cage?"

She glanced at it and smiled. "It's a terrarium, and it's mostly plants, but there's one Gulf Coast toad living in there. I've had him for a couple of years now."

Blake set what he was carrying on the coffee table and moved closer to look. Sure enough, hanging out inside a green mossy dome was a toad about four inches long. It turned its head to look back at him.

"That's really neat. I can't believe I didn't notice it last time. Do you have any other pets?"

"No. I'm at work too much to justify having a pet that actually needs personal attention." She chuckled and winced. "I'm going to run to the bathroom, change into more comfortable clothing, and then the recliner is calling my name."

He nodded. "Let me know if you need anything."

"Make yourself at home."

Blake ducked into the kitchen while she was gone. There were some dishes in the sink, and the counter was a little cluttered, but it was clean.

The kitchen had a watermelon theme down to the hand towels, cutting board, and even the salt and pepper shakers. It brought a smile to his face, just as it had the first time he'd seen it.

There were so many facets of Jenny's personality that were clicking into place. A few days ago, he never would've guessed she'd own an amphibian or that she liked watermelon so much, and yet it seemed to fit her perfectly.

He listened for Jenny, and when she returned, it was clear the events of the day were wearing on her. She cradled her side with one arm and carefully made a beeline for the recliner. "I found at the hospital that lying down was way less comfortable," she explained.

He held onto one arm and gently helped her sit down. The relief on her face was immediate. Without waiting for her to ask, he took the small blanket draped over the back of the couch and spread it over her lap. "Can I grab you something to drink?"

"A bottle of water from the fridge would be great. Thank you."

"No problem." By the time he returned with the water, Jenny's eyelids were drooping.

"I'm sorry I'm a lousy host. Help yourself to whatever's in the kitchen."

"I'll be fine. Get some rest."

The words were barely out of his mouth when her eyes

slid shut. Blake wanted so badly to reach out and brush a section of hair away from her face, but he was afraid he'd disturb her. Instead, he went to get himself a bottle of water and settle in at the dining room table.

It was six in the evening, and Jenny had been sleeping for a solid two hours. During that time, Blake sat at the kitchen table and caught up on his e-mail and social media, checked in with Walker, and ate a handful of mixed nuts from a jar on her kitchen counter along with an overly ripe banana.

He went into the living room when he heard her start to stir. She blinked several times and rubbed at her eyes.

"Hey. You stayed."

"Yep." He took a seat on the couch. "I'm glad you slept for a while. How are you feeling?"

"I think my head feels better." She looked at her watch and seemed surprised to see how much time had passed. "Did I miss anything?"

"Detective Walker said he and Bailey are going to swing by soon to drop my truck off and bring dinner. I have no idea what. He said they wouldn't come inside."

Jenny smiled. "Bailey has two little boys. She's probably afraid they'd get too riled up. That's sweet of them to bring food. And I'm sure you're ready to have your truck back."

He was, but mostly because he had a duffel bag with extra clothes and toiletries in it. He had no intention of leaving Jenny alone tonight to go back to the hotel, and she certainly wasn't up for the trip. But then again, there was no guarantee that she would let him stay there, either. That would ultimately have to be up to her.

"Do you want some more acetaminophen?"

"Please. I keep it in the first cabinet on the left as you go into the kitchen."

He retrieved the medication and handed it to her before regaining his spot on the couch.

After swallowing it, she set the bottle of water on the side table and leaned her head against the back of the chair. Her long, wavy hair pooled around her shoulders. As though she could sense his focus, she ran her fingers through her hair and twisted it, pulling it over one shoulder before letting it go again.

"Thank you for bringing me home and staying, Blake. After dinner, please feel free to go back to the hotel. I'm sure you'll be ready to rest and have some downtime by then."

"I really don't mind staying. If Walker's concerns about the shooter are right, God forbid, you aren't exactly at your best to deal with potential trouble. I can stay through tomorrow, drive you to the wedding, and go from there. At least, hopefully, we'll have caught the shooter, and you'll be feeling a lot better."

"That's not necessary, although I appreciate the offer. I'll get some rest tonight and be ready to go tomorrow."

By the way she didn't quite meet his eyes, even she knew that was a stretch.

"Jenny." He waited for her to look at him. "From what I know of you, you're quick to offer help to anyone and everyone who needs it. Why do you resist accepting help from someone else?"

She gave a dry laugh. "It's a character flaw I'm trying to work on."

"I wouldn't consider it a flaw so much as one of those invisible road bumps that catches you off guard. It's not like you haven't been through a lot in the last couple of days.

Truthfully, you should've gone with the chief's suggestion and taken next week off and rested up a little bit." The words were out before common sense had a chance to convince him to keep his mouth shut. He didn't regret it because what he said was true—even if it earned him a look of surprise that quickly morphed into annoyance.

She wadded up the blanket that had been resting on her lap and tossed it onto the couch next to Blake. "No offense, but I'm more than capable of knowing when I need to take time off. I plan on being out there Monday, looking for the suspect if they haven't been caught yet. I don't need a babysitter." Irritation flashed in her eyes. "We're not even on Grassle's detail anymore. You're free to go back to Austin anytime you're ready."

Now, she wasn't the only one who was irritated.

"I don't plan to leave Destiny until the person who shot you is in custody." His voice held a hint of anger, not at her but at the person who didn't seem to care who they hurt. He motioned to Jenny with one hand. "I watched my partner get shot and fall, not knowing if you were going to survive and wishing I were the one who had gone first to protect Grassle. Maybe you aren't the target, but I'm not about to walk away until we know that for sure."

Jenny absently scratched at the medical tape on her arm. She unwound it and then wrapped it around the piece of gauze beneath before tossing the ball of trash onto the side table. She said nothing, though, and it was difficult for him to know what she was thinking.

"Is that what you want me to do? Drive back to Austin tonight and not give a second thought to you or the case?"

She shrugged. Not exactly the direct answer he was hoping for. "I figured it might be what you wanted. It hasn't been the easiest of cases. Couple that with the fact that we don't always get along..." She tilted her head slightly as though she were waiting for him to acknowledge the truth of her words.

Blake could kick himself for all the times he'd teased her or been too hard on her. Apparently, he wasn't good at acting normal around a woman he was harboring feelings for. He ran a hand over the back of his neck and weighed his words carefully.

"For the record, when my boss brought up a job in Destiny, I specifically requested the assignment. I had no objections when I found out we'd be working together." He prayed she could read between the lines so he didn't have to spell it out for her. If she was going to laugh in his face or reject him, he'd rather it be after she drew her own conclusions instead of waiting until he'd told her how he felt directly.

There was no missing the shock on her face. Her mouth opened as though she were going to say something, but it snapped closed again.

When it didn't look like she was going to respond, Blake bit back a sigh. "Jenny? Next time there's an assignment in Destiny, do you want me to turn it down?"

Chapter Fifteen

Blake leaned forward to rest his elbows on his knees and watched Jenny closely. He didn't know how much more blunt he could be without telling her he cared about her and asking whether she felt the same way. A conversation neither of them were ready for.

Jenny reached for the ball of tape and gauze again and rolled it between her palms.

"You should take whatever assignments you want to take." She tried to go for casual, but she wasn't fooling Blake.

He wanted a black-and-white answer, not the kind women give because they want to stay neutral so they don't hurt someone else's feelings. "Answer the question, please. Do you want me to turn down the assignment next time?"

A growl emanated from her throat as she held the ball of tape between her thumb and first finger. "You are relentless." She lobbed it at him.

He deflected it effortlessly, and it fell on the cushion beside him. He was unable to hide his smile. "Yep."

She took a deep breath and let it out slowly. "I don't want you to turn down the assignment."

"Okay, then." He picked up the tape ball and handed it back to her, the tips of his fingers brushing hers.

"Okay, then." She accepted it and tossed it back onto the side table.

"For the record, I wasn't doubting your ability to do your job or take care of yourself. I've been where you are—coming off the adrenaline spike after taking one to the vest. The pain, frustration, fear. It all starts to blend together, and you're afraid that if you stop for five minutes, you won't be able to compartmentalize. Here's the thing, though. You're going to have to stop eventually, and you need to choose to do that before you push yourself too hard and don't have a choice." He hiked an eyebrow. "How close am I?"

"You're not entirely wrong." The words were barely audible.

"If you promise that you'll take time when you truly need it, I promise to stop bringing it up." He held out a hand. "Do we have a deal?"

"Agreed." She slipped her hand in his and gave it a hearty shake.

When she didn't immediately pull it away, he squeezed it gently.

"Can I stay through tomorrow? Take you to the wedding and then see how you're feeling when we get back?"

Her eyes narrowed, but there was a hint of a smile that curved the corners of her mouth. "You do like to push it, don't you?"

Blake shrugged. "Friends don't send injured friends to a wedding alone. Especially when they're potentially being hunted by a psychopath."

"When you put it that way..." Her gaze flitted from his

face to where their hands had shifted from a generic hand-shake to her petite hand resting in his.

He softly tapped her little finger with his thumb.

The doorbell rang, and he reluctantly let go of her hand and stood. "I'll make sure it's not your mom before I open it."

She chuckled and then groaned when her ribs must have protested.

Blake looked through the peephole to see a woman waiting with a large bag in her hands. Behind her, his truck was parked along the curb and another vehicle sat running.

He opened the door. "Hi. You must be Bailey."

"Yes, and you must be Blake." She smiled warmly. "It's nice to meet you. I wanted to drop this pasta off for you guys, give Jenny a quick hug, and then I'll be out of your hair. Nate's sitting in the car with the boys."

Walker waved from the other vehicle, and Blake returned the greeting.

"Of course, come on in." He closed the door behind her. "I can take that for you."

"Thank you."

As soon as the large paper bag was in his hands, the scent of chicken alfredo drifted to his nose. He breathed in deep, and his stomach growled in response. He set it on the counter in the kitchen before returning to the living room.

Bailey sat on the couch near Jenny, and the two women spoke easily for several minutes. It was clear they'd been friends for a while.

"If you need anything, just say the word. The boys and I can come help with housework or bring by a movie to watch. If you get bored, call me."

"I will."

Bailey stood again and gave Jenny a gentle hug. "Do me

a favor? Promise you won't take any unnecessary risks until everything gets sorted out."

Jenny gave an encouraging smile. "I promise."

"Good. You guys enjoy dinner. It was great to finally meet you, Blake."

"You, too." He escorted her out of the house and locked the door before returning to the living room. "Finally, huh? You've mentioned me?"

"In passing. Don't read too much into it."

They enjoyed pasta and rolls for dinner, and Jenny went to bed early. Blake offered to move her recliner into her room so she could sleep comfortably and have some privacy. She thankfully agreed. Once she turned in for the night, he tried to relax on the couch but had trouble sleeping at first. According to the doctor, there was no need to wake Jenny up in the middle of the night since her concussion was mild. It didn't keep him from worrying about her, though.

The next morning, she said her head felt better but that her ribs were quite sore. After a breakfast of scrambled eggs and bacon that Blake whipped together, she took a shower and had just returned when the doorbell rang, letting them know that Detective Walker was there to go over the details for the wedding on Saturday.

They sat in the living room where Walker was starting with an update on the case.

"One bullet was recovered from the scene of the shooting. It was a .45. The lab is still working on it, but so far, there has been no match to anything else in the system. Now, there were cameras scattered throughout the hotel, and that included the dining room where the purple backpack had been left. We got copies of the surveillance footage." He pulled a video up on his laptop and ran it for them.

They watched as a young girl carried the purple backpack into the room, looked around, and then set it on the floor in a corner. She left immediately.

"We were able to identify her and her family. She said that a tall man handed it to her, asked her to put it in the dining room, and gave her a five-dollar bill for her efforts."

Jenny's nostrils flared a little, and she pressed her lips together. "I hate it when criminals make kids do their dirty work. Cowards."

Blake couldn't agree more. "At least now we know we're looking for a male suspect." It wasn't a lot of help, but it was something. "Was the girl able to give any more of a description?"

"Not much. Tall. Wore a hat. She said he looked mean."

"Which is probably a big reason why she agreed to take the bag for him. Didn't want him to get angry." Jenny shook her head. "According to the time stamp on that video, the man who gave the girl the backpack would've had well over twelve minutes to get from there to his place in the building across from the hotel."

"He probably waited until he was in position before he called in the bomb threat," Walker agreed. "Unfortunately, we have no evidence to connect him to the bombing at the courthouse, even though my gut says this is the same person."

So did Blake's. "And no way to know for certain who the target was." Or why, if Jenny truly was the original target. How was he—or anyone else—supposed to protect her when they had so little information to go on?

"At this point, any connection to the death of Joseph

Kent at the courthouse and the bombing looks like a case of being in the wrong place at the wrong time. I don't think the gang member on trial was the target." Walker closed his laptop and set it aside. "We're still trying to find some kind of connection between the bombing and Grassle but haven't had much luck there, either. I'll be focusing on going through your past cases, Jenny, to see if there's anything that jumps out at me."

Jenny remained solemn, and Blake wondered if she was going through some of the cases she'd worked in her mind. "What about the wedding? Are we all set for tomorrow?"

"Yes, we're good to go. Officers Baker, Carrington, and Smith will be there in plainclothes. They'll make sure you both get earpieces, so you'll be alerted immediately if there's anything concerning. Between the three of them and Patterson being there with you, there shouldn't be a problem."

Blake prayed it would be as simple as that.

Chapter Sixteen

I t was mid-morning on Saturday when Jenny glanced at Blake sitting in the driver's seat of her car. She knew he would've preferred to drive his truck across town to her brother's wedding, but he insisted on taking her car because it was lower to the ground and easier for her to get in and out of. The kindness behind his reasoning hadn't escaped notice.

Not that she should be surprised. He'd been attentive and thoughtful all day yesterday, too. He'd commented on wanting to stay at her house through Saturday night. Part of her wanted to object, but both he and Nate had been right about one thing. She wasn't at her best. And while she still had difficulty grasping the idea that someone might be coming after her, she knew that if it were true, she wouldn't be at the top of her game. Having someone else nearby was the smart decision.

When she'd finally agreed to that yesterday, they'd taken her car to the hotel where he was staying so he could gather his things and check out. Then that afternoon, they'd talked about some of her old cases. She'd told him a little more about her family members so that he'd be better prepared for the wedding where he'd be meeting them all, and then they'd had fun visiting with Tia when she brought tacos by for dinner.

Now, it was Saturday, and they were on their way to the wedding. Jenny had let her parents know that Blake was coming along as a friend, but that didn't temper their excitement. Mom's squeal over the phone had been loud enough for Blake to hear.

Jenny prayed that most of the attention would be on Jared and Rita, where it should be, leaving Blake and Jenny to blend in a little more.

She glanced at his profile as he drove. He'd changed into a pair of navy slacks and paired them with a light blue, button-up, long-sleeved shirt that somehow highlighted the blue in his hazel eyes. Handsome didn't even begin to describe the man. No, this guy wasn't going to fade into the background; that much was sure. On the contrary, she might have to knock women away from him with the small handbag she'd brought.

Jenny's fingers itched at the memory of Blake holding her hand the other night. At least, that's what she thought was happening when Bailey had arrived at the house. Even with all the time they spent together yesterday and this morning, nothing like that had happened again. She was starting to wonder if she'd imagined it.

Maybe it would have been better if she had. Talk about complicating things. Blake lived in Austin, and that's where he'd be going back to as soon as this case wrapped up. It was nearly a year between the last time she'd seen him and now. It was likely to be just as long or longer until the next time. Then again, Austin and Destiny were only an hour and a half apart. That wasn't that far.

"You okay over there?"

Blake's voice startled her, and she shook her runaway thoughts from her head.

"Yeah, sorry. Preoccupied, I guess." She glanced at him again, and her face flushed.

"You look beautiful, Jenny. I should've told you that earlier. Everything is going to be fine today."

She looked down at the long, navy-blue dress she'd chosen a couple of months back. It was comfortable. The skirt flowed to her calves, and the sleeves were long, which she appreciated for a December wedding. Ironically, it now looked like she and Blake had planned to match each other today.

"Thank you. You clean up nicely yourself."

"Why, thank you." He flashed her a grin that made her heart tumble over itself. "The exit should be right up here, I think."

"Yes, on the right. You'll see a sign... there."

Felicity Grove was gorgeous. Even in the winter, when most of the trees were bare, it was like something straight out of a storybook.

"Wow, you weren't kidding when you said this place was fancy. I truly had no idea there was someplace like this the first time I came into Destiny." Blake followed other cars down a winding road leading to a large building that looked like a colonial-style mansion. "Impressive."

"The wedding will be outside in the garden area, but they're holding the reception inside next to the dance hall."

It was nice that everything was all in one location. There were also only two ways on and off the property, which would make it easier to keep an eye on things. Jenny was glad to know that other officers were going to be present, even if only she and Blake were aware of the fact.

They parked, and Blake came around to help her out. As they walked to the front of the building where everyone seemed to be headed, Blake's hand stayed at the small of her back.

Officer Mari Smith met them with a smile. She discretely handed each of them an earpiece, reassured them that everything was under control, and blended right back into the crowd.

Blake popped his into his ear. Jenny did the same and used her fingers to comb her hair on that side and bring it to the front. She turned to face Blake. "It's pretty visible, isn't it?" She couldn't imagine being able to hide it well with all the hugs she anticipated from family members.

He reached up and rubbed a section of her hair between his fingers. "Yep. We're not going to need these, anyway. It's just a precaution. Put yours in your bag so you'll have it, and I'll listen in. Everyone here will assume I've got the game on or something." He took the device out of her ear and handed it to her.

Jenny dropped it into her bag like he'd suggested. He gave her an encouraging smile and held an elbow out to escort her. She slipped her arm through it and rested her hand on his bicep. When he covered it with his own, it took a lot of focus to ignore the instinct to lean into him.

The next hour flew by as Jenny must have introduced Blake as a friend two dozen times to siblings, cousins, aunts, and uncles.

Mom had no problem giving him a hug. Dad, on the other hand, was friendly and welcoming while obviously sizing Blake up. Dad finally tapped his ear and turned his head to reveal he had an AirPod nestled in one ear. "NBA or NHL?"

"Always been a hockey fan myself. Saw a few Stars games with my dad some years back."

"Good man."

Jenny watched in amazement as Blake and her dad easily conversed about sports, and never once did Blake say he was actually listening to a game. Her parents moved away, giving them a moment of peace before Aunt Cindy wandered over to say hello.

The wedding ceremony itself was beautiful. Jenny had had her doubts about a winter wedding, but Felicity Grove pulled it off spectacularly. When Jared and Rita were presented as husband and wife, Jenny couldn't stop the joyful tears.

The last of her siblings was now married, and they all seemed so happy. She was thrilled for them; truly, she was, but it was impossible not to feel left behind at the same time.

As if he sensed her conflicting emotions, Blake placed a supporting hand against her back. The warmth seeped through the fabric of her dress to her skin, a direct contrast to the cool air surrounding them.

The newly married couple waved to their friends and family and then walked, arm in arm, back down the aisle as everyone cheered and clapped.

Blake's arm suddenly went around Jenny's waist and tightened. Her gaze jumped to his face to find him pressing his earpiece to activate the microphone. "Understood. We're going in now."

Chapter Seventeen

People began to fill the aisle as they followed the new bride and groom into the building. Jenny's body tensed as Blake directed her toward the door, his arm still around her waist. She fished in her bag for the earpiece and put it in.

Baker's voice came through immediately. "...took off through the kitchen. I'm in pursuit."

"I'm outside and going around the back," Smith answered.

Once inside, Blake led her to a large changing room off to one side. He closed and locked the door behind him.

"What's going on?"

"There's a disturbance near the kitchen. It's probably just a couple of caterers coming to blows, but we're taking precautions until we know for sure."

Her gun was in a holster around her thigh. She patted it through the skirt of her dress and took comfort knowing she had it if necessary. Situations like this were exactly why she never left the house without it.

Baker's voice came over the coms. "Situation is under

control. I repeat, the situation is under control. We are in the clear."

Jenny released a lungful of air and leaned against the wall. It was only then that she realized how sore her ribs were from walking around and being on her feet all day.

A moment later, Carrington said, "It was an escalation of an ongoing dispute between two brothers who work for the catering company. There's quite a mess, but the wedding party shouldn't be affected."

"Thanks, everyone." Jenny tapped her earpiece to turn off the microphone. Thank goodness none of the mess was going to ruin Jared and Rita's reception. She thought of something and started to laugh, which immediately had her bracing her side.

Blake turned off his microphone as well. He approached her with a smile on his face but a flash of concern in his eyes. "What's so funny?"

"Can you imagine the brothers' surprise when their dispute brought in two undercover officers? I wish I could've seen it." She laughed harder, and the combination of that and the pain brought tears to her eyes. With a groan, she leaned the back of her head against the wall.

He chuckled and reached out to put a hand on her arm. "You need to stop that. You're making *my* side hurt."

"I'm just glad everything is okay."

"Yeah, me, too."

Suddenly, the mood in the room shifted and the humor dissipated. In its place was a crackle of awareness that seemed to arc between them. She swallowed hard, mindful of the fact they were alone together and that he was still touching her arm.

Blake took another step forward, his shoes nearly

touching hers. "Has anyone told you that you have a beautiful laugh?" His voice came out husky.

She shook her head, suddenly self-conscious. Well, she was sure her parents probably told her that at some point in her life. No one else ever had.

"That's a shame because it is." There was not even a hint of humor in his expression now. Instead, he seemed to be studying her face. Searching for something specific. "*You* are truly beautiful."

He reached out to brush some of her hair back and let his thumb linger against her cheek. He hesitated for a heartbeat before he leaned in and brushed a kiss against her cheek.

Jenny's heart thrummed in her ears as he pressed another whisper of a kiss to the corner of her mouth. At that moment, all she wanted him to do was kiss her again. She pressed the palm of her hand to his chest, satisfied to feel that his heart was racing like hers was.

This time, when Blake leaned in, his lips covered hers. The intensity of the sensations took her breath as a cocoon of safety enveloped her. She wrapped her arm around his neck, and he deepened the kiss just as someone pounded on the door.

"We're all clear. You guys are good to come out," Officer Smith called through the door.

Jenny's face heated, and she rested her forehead against his chest with a groan.

She should get out there and rejoin the reception before someone came looking for her. The last thing she needed was for one of her family members to catch them in here. News would spread through her family in ten minutes flat.

Blake stepped back, allowing her room to push away from the wall. Together, they walked to the door and opened it. Jenny prayed her face didn't look as red as it felt. She dropped her earpiece back into her bag.

Mari Smith didn't seem to think anything of it as she waved them out. "They're taking photos of the wedding party, and everyone else is in the dining room. The bride and groom will be joining you all shortly."

"Thank you. All of you." Jenny was sincerely grateful that they'd been there and reacted so quickly.

"You're welcome. Here's hoping that'll be the only excitement of the evening." She turned and headed back to wherever she was, keeping an eye on things.

Jenny knew what Mari meant, but the debacle in the kitchen was most definitely not the only excitement.

She was thankful to have a lot to distract her from the headache that was beginning to form in the back of her head, her aching ribs, and the kiss she couldn't stop thinking about. Even though she really wasn't very hungry, she ate some food so she could take another dose of medication and prayed it would kick in quickly.

They were sitting at a round table when the dancing began. Jenny watched as Jared and Rita began their first dance together as husband and wife. When the song was over, they invited everyone else to join them if they'd like.

The rest of their table cleared out, leaving Jenny and Blake sitting alone. It didn't take long before Mom came flitting up. "Wasn't that first dance beautiful? I had my doubts about a winter wedding, but this has been gorgeous."

"It really has," Jenny agreed. "Can you imagine how beautiful this place would be in the spring?"

Mom pressed a hand to her chest and just shook her head. "Now, why aren't the two of you out there dancing?"

"I told you, Mom, Blake and I just came as friends." Apparently, friends who kiss, but she didn't need to know that. Jenny hadn't even been able to fully process that fact yet herself.

"And friends can't dance together? Nonsense. Your father and I were best friends long before we fell in love. Trust me, that's how the best love stories start." She gave them an exaggerated wink and floated off into the crowd.

She dared to look at Blake and found him already watching her. "I'm game if you feel up to it."

It'd practically be a crime not to. She nodded and instantly regretted the motion when her head throbbed. She stood and took his outstretched hand.

The song was slow, sweet, and perfect. Blake held her close as they swayed to the music with the other couples on the dance floor. She rested her cheek against his shoulder.

"Jenny?" He spoke with a low voice near her ear.

She shivered. "Yeah?"

When she raised her head to look at him, and a bright light from across the room caught her eye, she immediately flinched.

"Is your head bothering you again?"

"I took more medication, but so far, it isn't doing much."

Blake glanced around them. "It's no wonder. Why don't I take you home so you can rest?"

"That actually sounds wonderful. I just need to tell Jared and Rita goodbye. My parents, too. Then we can go."

"Okay. I'll let Carrington and the others know as well."

They all seemed to understand when she told them she wasn't feeling well. By the time she was free to leave, it was getting dark outside. Jenny welcomed the dimmer lighting and wished she could close her eyes right then and there.

"You have to stay awake long enough to get in the car," Blake told her as he took her hand in his. "Once we leave, the others are going to head home, too."

"That will work out well." Jenny focused on the feel of his palm against hers and her car up ahead that was taking entirely too long to reach.

When she finally collapsed in the passenger seat and put her seat belt on, she breathed a sigh of relief. She wasn't sure if she'd ever been this tired before.

Blake got behind the wheel. "Try to get some rest. I'll wake you up when we get back to your house."

She nodded once and closed her eyes.

The next thing she knew, Blake was gently shaking her shoulder. "We're here, Jenny."

"Where?" She forced her eyes open and groaned.

He chuckled. "Your house. Come on, let's get you inside before I'm forced to carry you in." He got out and went around to open her door. She was thankful for his help getting out of the car. There was no doubt in her mind that she'd be even more sore tomorrow.

They were halfway up the walkway when she got the feeling they were being watched. She cast a glance behind them and then focused on the house again. She'd forgotten to close all the curtains, making it easy to see inside the house now that it was dark. Except that the first front curtain had been drawn. A chill ran down her spine.

"Blake." She tugged him to a stop. "The front curtain is closed. I didn't close it before we left. Did you?"

Blake let go of her hand and reached for his weapon. "No, I didn't."

Chapter Eighteen

Blake was vaguely aware of Jenny reaching under her skirt and withdrawing her gun. Even with them both armed, he didn't like the idea that someone could be watching them. He was tempted to ask her to go back and wait in the car, but as an officer, she wouldn't want to do that, and he'd feel the same way if roles were reversed. He wasn't about to split up either, though.

"I'm calling for backup." With her gun in her right hand, she used her left to dig the phone out of her bag. She dropped the bag on the ground to dial a number and hold the phone to her ear. "Hey, this is Durant. There may be an intruder in my house. Agent Patterson and I are requesting an additional unit."

Blake motioned to the right of the house. He wanted to get a look inside using one of the other windows. Jenny nodded her agreement. They walked along until they reached the side of the house. She stopped there with the phone still up to her ear waiting to relay anything he saw.

He crouched down and crept up to the windows, his gun at the ready. Cautiously, he rose enough to look through and into the well-lit living room. He didn't see anyone inside, and nothing seemed out of place. If someone had been in the house, at least they hadn't ransacked it. Something caught his eye, and he focused on the front door, which was visible from where he stood. Wires led to a small box resting on the floor just inside.

The door had been wired with explosives.

He turned on his heel and ran toward Jenny. "Get away from the house! There's a bomb inside." Blood pounded in his ears as adrenaline surged through him.

Her eyes flew wide, and she immediately ran back toward the street with him on her six. When they got to the car, he held his hand out for her phone.

"This is Agent Patterson. We're going to need a bomb squad at Officer Durant's house. The front door is rigged with explosives."

"Copy that. Units are en route."

He handed the phone back to Jenny who hung up and put it on the hood of the car.

She shivered. "What if he's out here somewhere?"

"I don't like this, either." He needed to get her off the street, but there wasn't much he could do until the others arrived.

Thankfully, they didn't have long to wait. Two police cars pulled up, quickly followed by a third. Officer Lorenzo and another guy Blake didn't know started to suit up. Only then did he and Jenny lower their weapons.

Detective Paris jogged over. "Walker is on his way in. I guess there's no doubt now who this guy is after." He eyed Jenny. "We need to get you out of the open. Patterson, take her back to the precinct. We'll keep you guys updated."

Jenny leaned against the car. What energy she'd had earlier seemed to drain out of her completely.

Paris must have noticed. "Eve's working late tonight. I'll let her know you're coming. She's got that couch in the visitor's room where you'll have some quiet. Why don't you try to get some rest while we get this taken care of?"

When she nodded her agreement and moved to get in the car, Blake knew she was exhausted. He clapped Paris on the shoulder. "You guys be safe. We'll be waiting to hear from you."

"You got it."

Blake jogged around the car and got in behind the wheel. Jenny leaned her head against the window and said nothing. She had to be worried about her fellow officers, and the possibility that she might lose her house had to be a concern as well. There was little he could say to make her feel better, so he opted for prayer instead.

"Father God, we pray for Your protection over Lorenzo, Paris, and the other officers working at the house right now. Give them wisdom as they disarm the bomb. Please lead us to the person responsible so we can stop him before someone else gets hurt. Thank You, God, for keeping Jenny and me safe. Give Jenny peace as she waits for word on her house and help her to get some rest in the meantime. Thank You for Your unending grace and love. Amen."

"Amen," she echoed. She covered a yawn as they pulled into the parking lot at the precinct. "I'm so tired, Blake. Mentally and physically."

He parked and went around to her side of the car. He opened the door and helped her out. "I know, sweetheart. Let's get you inside. Who's Eve, and where is her office? Paris was right. You need to lie down for a while."

"Eve is the medical examiner. She and Detective Paris are engaged. They're supposed to be getting married sometime next summer."

"Wow, I had no idea." He was glad he could keep her talking and hopefully distracted, even if only a little. "I wouldn't have thought of the morgue as a comfortable place to rest."

She chuckled. "Right? There's a nice family room for the relatives of the deceased—for when they come in to identify a loved one. There are a couple of couches in there, and it's really cozy. Comforting."

She told him which direction to go now that they were inside and pressed a hand to the side of her head. Her progress was slowing, so he looped an arm around her waist to give her some support.

They entered a hallway, and he spotted the sign for the morgue ahead on the left. A woman with red hair and striking green eyes swung the door open before he had a chance to knock.

"Come on in." She closed and locked the door behind her and extended a hand toward Blake. "I'm Eve Marks. You must be Agent Patterson. John texted ahead to let me know the situation." She turned her attention to Jenny and gave her a gentle hug. "You look like you're about ready to drop. Come on, I've got the room ready for you."

"Thanks, Eve. I appreciate it."

They followed her to a nearby room where a pillow and blankets had been placed on the couch. A bottle of water sat nearby, and the lights had been dimmed.

"I wish I could offer you a change of clothes, but that's something I don't have."

"This is perfect. Thank you." She looked longingly at the bed. "I feel horrible for lying down and sleeping with everything that's going on."

"I know. We all know. Sometimes, the body decides for us what we need, and there's not much we can do about it.

Get some rest." She turned to Blake. "I'll be in my office for the next few hours. Feel free to stop by."

He gave her a nod, then helped Jenny to the couch. He pulled the blankets back and waited for her to lie down and get comfortable before covering her.

She slid an arm under the pillow and laid her head down with a sigh. "Promise me you'll wake me up with any news?"

"I promise." He leaned over and pressed a kiss to her forehead. "Get some rest. Your phone's right here by the water. I'll be nearby if you need me."

She nodded. Within moments, her breathing evened out as sleep claimed her.

Blake took in a deep breath. It was no wonder they had no issues at the wedding. The guy had been at Jenny's place.

For the first time since they'd arrived at her house and he'd seen the explosives, he allowed himself to think about what might have happened if Jenny hadn't noticed the curtain. The bomber must have closed it so no one would see him rigging the explosives, and then he forgot to open it again. That one little mistake might have saved their lives.

Chapter Nineteen

The room spun slowly as Jenny relaxed in Blake's arms. They were the only couple on the dance floor at her brother's wedding. A crowd of people watched them from the sidelines. She could tell they were smiling, but the faces themselves were a blur.

The feeling of safety and love evaporated as a chill, like a drop of ice water, pricked the back of her neck and traveled down her spine. Instinctively, Jenny knew that someone else was watching them. Someone who wasn't happy to see them dancing. They spun faster and faster as Jenny craned her neck and tried to spot the person who was so angry with them.

There! It was a man on the edge of the crowd. She couldn't quite make out his features, but there was no missing the hatred in his eyes.

That's when his mouth stretched into an unnaturally wide grin as he raised a gun and pointed it right at them—

Jenny's eyes flew open, and she gripped the arms of her recliner. It took several seconds to realize she was in her bedroom at home. It was still dark outside, and the house was quiet. She glanced at the clock on the side table over by her bed. It was almost seven o'clock. It felt so much earlier thanks to the late sunrises this time of the year.

The bomb squad had dismantled the bomb at the front door and swept the rest of the house for any other explosives. The bomber had gained access to the house through a side window. The entire pane of glass was broken. Someone made sure the window was boarded up until she could get a repairman to come out and replace it on Monday.

She and Blake were finally cleared to go back in around one in the morning. Even after sleeping for a couple of hours in the family room near Eve's office, she still had no problem falling asleep again once she was back in her own home.

Her mind and body might've thought she felt safe, but that nightmare said differently. Knowing someone intent on killing her had been wandering through her house creeped her out. Too bad she didn't have a dog. The hours she spent at the station, though, would make her feel guilty for leaving the poor thing alone at the house so much.

Then again, maybe having a dog would encourage her to go home earlier and more often. Plus, it would be nice to not be alone. It was something to consider once they got this case wrapped up and the bomber behind bars.

At least she wasn't alone now. Her thoughts drifted to Blake. Knowing that he was in the living room erased any anxiety left behind by her bad dreams.

That kiss yesterday at the wedding had been amazing. Just thinking about it sent her heart rate into overdrive. It was weird to think that, a week ago, she'd dreaded having to work with him again. And now? She hated the idea of him heading back to Austin.

It was proof of how much could change in a few days' time.

Jenny lifted the blanket off her lap and carefully got up. To her surprise and relief, there was no headache at all. While her ribs were still sore, there was obvious improvement in that area, too. Encouraged, she gathered her things and headed into the bathroom for a shower before getting dressed for the day.

By the time she got out, she had a text message from Bailey waiting for her.

> Hey, we were hoping to come by around nine. We thought we'd bring breakfast and fellowship to you since you can't get to church. Several others would like to join us. Let me know if that's okay.

The message brought a smile to Jenny's face. Normally, she'd go to church and then swing by and have lunch with her parents or something. She'd already messaged them and let them know she wouldn't be there.

The fact that her friends had thought of her warmed her heart.

With her hair still damp, Jenny softly opened her door in case Blake was still sleeping. She found him sitting at the table in the kitchen with a cup of coffee.

"Good morning," he greeted with a smile. "How are you feeling this morning?"

He'd done some laundry yesterday morning and was now wearing the dark green polo shirt he'd been wearing the first day he'd arrived in Destiny. Even then, when she was annoyed to see him, she'd had to admit it looked good on him.

"Good. Much better, actually." She poured herself a

cup of coffee, added sugar and cream, then went to sit down across from him, inhaling the heavenly scent. "Thanks for making coffee. Did you sleep okay?"

"For the most part. It took a little while to settle down after all the adrenaline. How about you?" He took a sip of his coffee and eyed her over the rim of his cup.

Did she look tired, or had she spoken in her sleep last night? She hoped not the latter. "I had nightmares. I guess that's to be expected." Jenny shrugged as though it were no big deal and took a sip of her own coffee. Exactly what she needed. "Bailey and Nate want to come by at nine. A couple of other people from the precinct want to join them. Are you okay with that?"

He seemed surprised by the question. "Sure. It's your home, Jenny. You don't have to run things by me."

Her face warmed a little. "Maybe not, but I didn't know if you had any plans to go to the precinct. I wouldn't mind going and looking through old cases myself if someone can keep an eye on the house while we're gone."

A regular patrol going by or even sitting outside the house should be enough to deter someone from breaking in again. It might be safer to stay at the house, but she couldn't sit around and wait. She simply wasn't wired that way.

"That sounds like a great idea. Even if we could get some of the digital case files sent to us here, there would be a lot of others that we'd be missing. I imagine most older cases are still stored in paper format."

"Yes, they are. In theory, going all digital would be nice, but it's very time-consuming to go back through and update everything."

She texted Bailey back to let her know that would be fine.

When she looked up again, she found Blake watching her, a small smile on his face.

"What?" Jenny swiped at her mouth in case she had a coffee mustache going on or something.

He chuckled. "It's nothing bad. I was just admiring your freckles. They're really pretty."

She automatically touched the bridge of her nose. As a child, she used to hate the light-brown freckles that dotted her nose and her cheeks. As the only one in her family to have them, she saw them as blemishes. Her parents told her they were beautiful, and she'd come to accept them and even forget they were there. She'd never seen them as an especially good thing—until now.

"Thank you."

"You're welcome." He reached across the small table and covered her hand with his own. "About yesterday... I wanted you to know that—"

His cell phone rang, the vibration causing it to move on the table where it sat.

Blake glanced at the screen and sighed. "It's my boss. He tried to get a hold of me last night, and I didn't see the call until much later. I need to take this." With an apologetic look and a gentle squeeze of her hand, he swiped to answer and moved to the living room to talk.

Jenny made herself busy washing the few dishes in the sink and tidying up the kitchen. She could hear Blake's voice but couldn't make out what he was saying.

She'd just hung up the hand towel when he came back in again with a discouraged look on his face.

"What's wrong?"

"I'm needed back in Austin by tomorrow morning." He raked his fingers through his hair. "With us no longer on Grassle's detail and her giving her testimony tomorrow, my boss sees no reason for me to stay in town when there are other cases I should be working on."

Jenny's heart sank. Realistically, she knew that he would have to go back eventually. But tomorrow? It seemed so soon. She wasn't ready for him to leave.

Chapter Twenty

The disappointment on Jenny's face made Blake feel horrible. The last thing he wanted to do was leave her while they were still trying to find the person who'd tried to kill her more than once. He'd be tempted to take some leave and stay, but short-notice vacations like that wouldn't fly right now. They were down two agents in their office already: one absence due to an injury, and the other was on paternity leave.

At the same time, seeing Jenny's immediate sadness at his news gave him hope. If she was even half as disappointed as he was about him leaving Destiny and not seeing her every day, then maybe they could figure out a way to change that—at least get to know each other better. He could drive the hour and a half to Destiny on a Friday night, or even stay at a hotel over the weekend.

Jenny nodded and averted her eyes. "It makes sense that they'd want you back there. I'm sure there's more than one case that they'd like you to work."

"Maybe. I'd really prefer not to leave until this case is closed, though. The thought that someone is still after you and I won't be here to help doesn't sit right with me." Thankfully, she had a whole police department behind her. He knew they'd do their best to protect her, and there was some solace in that.

"Then we'll have to pray that we catch this guy today." She squared her shoulders. "We'll figure this out." She lifted her chin then, and a flicker of uncertainty told him that she was just as confused by this change in their relationship as he was and that she was referring to more than just the case.

"Yes, we will." He took several steps forward and gently wrapped his arms around her.

When she leaned in and held him back, he knew he'd made the right decision. He rested his cheek against her damp hair, breathed in the scent of her shampoo, and desperately wished for a future where he got to do this every day. He said a silent prayer that God would give them both wisdom moving forward.

After several moments, he stepped back and cradled her cheek with one of his hands. "Jenny, you should know that kissing you yesterday... was something I've wanted to do for a long time. I don't know where you're at right now, but I wanted to make it clear that it wasn't just because we were locked in a room together or the stress. At least it wasn't for me."

She grasped his wrist and rose to her tiptoes. Without a word, she pressed her lips to his in a whisper of a kiss that took all his doubts and kicked them right out the window. They smiled at each other before he pulled her close and kissed her again. Knowing that she felt the same way made this kiss even sweeter.

A car door shut outside. Blake broke the kiss and rested his forehead against hers. "If that's Smith again, I'm going to suspect a conspiracy."

Jenny chuckled and took a step back. She fanned her face, ran her fingers through her hair to straighten it again, and took a deep breath. "We're going to be surrounded by officers and at least one detective."

"Right." He tugged on his shirt to make sure it was straight and flashed her a grin. "Law enforcement mode activated."

She laughed again before turning to the door and looking through the peep hole. Smiling, she swung the door open.

"Jenny!" An adorable little boy ran in and oh-so-gently hugged Jenny. His parents must've warned him to be careful with her cracked ribs. Another boy, who was a year or two younger followed along with a Rottweiler who seemed as happy to be there as the kids.

"Hey, guys. Are you behaving yourselves?"

The younger boy shook his head, causing Blake to laugh out loud.

Jenny ruffled the boy's hair. "Well, Jordan, at least you're honest." She hugged Bailey and Detective Walker as they came in before reaching down to pet the dog.

Walker balanced two large boxes of donuts in one arm and held a hand toward Blake. "Good to see you."

"You too, detective."

"It's Nate," he said with a smile. "These two rambunctious boys are Seth and Jordan. Guys, this is Mr. Blake." He put a hand up to his mouth as though he were revealing a great secret. "And it's a shame that they don't like donuts."

"Yes, we do!"

"I do, too, like donuts!"

Their reactions had all the adults laughing.

Blake shook each of the boys' hands. "It's good to meet you both. And I like donuts, too."

The Rottweiler wandered over and sat right in front of Blake as though she were waiting for her introduction. Blake offered a hand and was rewarded with a lick.

Nate laughed. "And that's Minnie, friend to all. Well, almost everyone, anyway."

The doorbell rang again, and Jenny ushered Tia in carrying two drink carriers full of to-go cups of coffee. Behind her came Officer Josh Carrington and a woman holding a baby boy. Carrington took one of the drink carriers from Tia. The last people to enter were Officer Clint Baker, who was carrying a large box that he set down on the coffee table, and Logan Alcott, the station's tech guru.

It was quickly obvious that these people were close friends and that everyone went by their first names. Blake was thankful that Jenny had that kind of support.

Josh shook Blake's hand. "This is Penny Hughes, my fiancée."

He nodded at the petite brunette. "It's nice to meet you."

"It's nice to meet you, too. This is my foster son, Ben." She jiggled the baby, who gave Blake a gummy grin.

Tia looked around the room. "I wasn't sure what everyone preferred in their coffee, so these are all black, and you can add what you want."

"I'll get the sugar and creamers out." Bailey left for the kitchen.

Blake had quickly learned once he started working with the Destiny Police Department that their coffee was some of the best he'd ever had. Everyone credited Tia for that, and he wondered where she got it from and if she'd share her secret with his FBI office.

He glanced at Jenny to find her standing in the middle

of the living room, a look of wonder on her face. "You are all amazing. Thank you for coming over."

"Are you kidding? Where two or more are gathered in His name... Today, we gather here at your house." Penny reached out and gave Jenny's hand a squeeze.

For the next hour, the house was perfectly noisy with the sounds of people laughing and conversing. The two boxes of donuts didn't last long, and soon, young Seth and Jordan were full of sugar-induced energy.

To Blake's surprise, Jenny asked him to move the large box to the floor, and then she lifted the top of the treasure chest coffee table. There were all kinds of toys, from puzzles to action figures, plush animals to baby toys. She waved the little boys over and allowed them to choose a toy to play with.

Jenny clearly not only had people over to her house regularly, but she was prepared to entertain even the youngest of her guests.

She found a set of large, plastic keys and held them out to baby Ben, who eagerly grabbed them and shoved the red one in his mouth. Jenny looked longingly at the baby and gave him a wave before finding a spot on the couch and gingerly lowering herself into one corner. Penny joined her.

Nate sat on the floor and helped the boys put together a Hot Wheels track. He moved it into the kitchen, where the youngsters took a dozen cars and decided to race them systematically to see which one was the fastest.

Blake enjoyed visiting with everyone and seeing how easily they all relaxed around each other. It was especially interesting to watch the interactions between the couples. Josh was never far from Penny and the baby and regularly checked to see if they needed anything, while Nate and

Bailey kept seeking each other out across the room and smiling.

Coming from a childhood where his parents would sooner yell at each other than have a polite conversation, this was all fairly new to Blake. This was what he wanted, though. Some day. His gaze flitted to Jenny.

Nate stood and walked over to Bailey and squeezed her hand. She raised her voice enough to be heard above the various conversations in the room. "Tia and Penny, why don't we go into the kitchen and see if there's any coffee left?"

Jenny smiled at Ben, who had fallen asleep in his foster mother's arms. Penny stood carefully to not wake him.

When everyone who wasn't a police officer left the room, Clint lifted the box and put it back on the coffee table. "We took the liberty of bringing in a bunch of your old cases, Jenny."

Logan took a laptop out of a case he'd brought with him. "We thought if we worked together, we could narrow down a list of suspects to investigate."

Chapter Twenty-One

The kindness of her friends was nearly overwhelming. Jenny didn't know what she'd do without the people gathered in her home, and that included Blake. Together, they systematically went through the old case files, and then Logan searched the suspects' current locations.

Jenny handed the final case file over to Clint, who packed it back in the box. She shifted her weight again and settled into the corner of the couch. Every once in a while, they could hear the others from the kitchen. Jenny wished she'd been able to hold and rock baby Ben. Normally, she would've snatched him right up as soon as Penny brought him in, but she knew her ribs would've protested.

She prayed that, someday, she'd have a child of her own. It'd always seemed like this distant possibility, which was more of a dream than a reality, until now.

Earlier, when she'd been talking to the baby, she'd glanced at Blake to find he was watching her with a soft expression on his face. What about him? Did he want a family? Kids?

It was probably silly to even be wondering about that right now. So, they'd kissed. Twice. That didn't exactly put them on the track to marriage. There was a lot she still didn't know about him. They lived in different towns, and both had jobs that were time-consuming and, at times, dangerous.

All of those were good reasons to doubt that anything serious between them could last. Right now, though, it gave her hope. Which, on the relationship front, was more than she'd had in a long time.

As if he somehow sensed someone was thinking about him, Ben's wail drifted in from the dining room.

Josh chuckled. "He probably just woke up. The little guy wakes up acting like he's starving to death. Every single time." He left to go check on them.

"Okay," Nate began, "let's go over our top three suspects quickly and then set this aside so the rest of our group can come back out. I can imagine it's a bit of a circus in there."

Josh returned, bringing with him a whiff of something baking. "Yep. Everyone seems to be having fun, though. Looks like they're making cookies." He patted his belly appreciatively.

Murmurs of approval echoed around the room.

Jenny loved that her friends felt comfortable enough to find everything in her kitchen like that. She only wished that there wasn't a case this dire so she could be in there baking with them.

Nate cleared his throat. "All right. First up, we have Carlton Malone. He was just released from prison on parole last month after serving six years."

It took a moment for Logan to pull Malone's image up on his laptop. He turned it around so they could all see it.

"He's been involved in multiple cases of domestic disturbance, and several women filed charges against him for abusive behavior that were eventually dropped. What landed him in jail was assault with a deadly weapon. He broke into his ex-girlfriend's house with a baseball bat to her sliding glass door and then proceeded to use it to take his anger out on her." Nate frowned as he looked at his notes. "Thankfully, she wasn't alone at the time."

Jenny remembered the guy. She was one of the officers who showed up on the scene after the woman's brother called it in. He'd been the one staying with her, and Malone had come out on the losing end of that encounter. "Jadlowski and I responded to the scene. Even after taking a pretty good beating from the woman's brother, Malone had a lot of adrenaline and rage. He obviously had an issue with women because my ears are still ringing from all the profanity he flung my way."

"Maybe he took it personally that you were one of the officers who put him away," Josh suggested.

Blake clenched his jaw. "A lot of times, men who have issues with women tend to hold a grudge."

"True. But I wasn't even the one who cuffed him. I sat with his ex while we waited for the ambulance." It didn't make sense for the guy to harbor hatred for Jenny, but then, sometimes nothing made sense when it came to the violence that one human being could inflict on another.

"I think it's worth questioning him." Nate looked at Blake and Jenny. "Why don't the two of you interview him? If he *is* the bomber, he won't expect you to come knocking on his front door. Plus, you can gauge how he reacts to seeing you, Jenny. Has he been harboring hatred, or will he even recognize you?"

"That sounds good." Jenny glanced at Blake, who gave a solemn nod.

Logan started typing on his computer. "I'm sending that address and the details to your phones now."

Clint spoke up from his spot on the couch. "Next, we have an Angelo Sandoval. Originally from Houston, he came into Destiny with an influx of fentanyl. Jenny, you were part of the large undercover operation that eventually landed him in jail, and you testified at his hearing."

Logan turned his computer around to show them the man's mugshot. "Unfortunately, some of the evidence was dismissed, and he only received three years in jail before being released last week. I have an address for him in Destiny, but he had a lot of connections in Houston as well."

Jenny doubted the guy would've gone through his prison sentence focused on her when there were so many other people involved in that operation. Then again, up until a week ago, she couldn't imagine anyone wanting to kill her at all.

"I'll try to get a hold of Sandoval first. Reach out to any of his old contacts and see what he's been up to. Get a list of people from the trial and name them, along with Jenny, and see if he reacts." Nate made some more notes. "And our last guy isn't directly related to Jenny at all."

"I took the initiative and ran a search for individuals with a criminal record and a history of either pyromania or explosives. One name came up." Logan showed them an image of a man in his late twenties. "Martin Johnson has been in and out of trouble since he was a teenager. He was accused multiple times of setting a fire out of anger, although there was never enough evidence to actually charge him for it. Previous investigations have turned up material on his computer that's questionable at best, including instructions on how to build explosives."

Clint nodded. "I remember this guy. The last time he was arrested, it was because he'd allegedly been planning to bomb one of the local department stores because they refused to let him return something he claimed he bought there. A friend called in an anonymous tip. But since there was no physical bomb or any evidence that all of it had been discussed, we couldn't hold him."

Blake leaned forward to get a better look at the picture. "But there's no connection to Jenny?"

"I don't remember ever seeing him or meeting him," she said.

"None that I could find," Logan confirmed.

"Jenny and I could find and question him, too. See if he reacts to seeing her." Blake looked to Nate to see if he agreed.

Nate regarded Jenny. "Are you sure you're up to it?"

"Absolutely." She was still tired, and her ribs ached, but she felt a lot better than she had yesterday. "I can't just sit and wait around for this guy to try something else."

Chapter Twenty-Two

Blake didn't particularly care for the idea of Jenny being out in the open. Not to mention the doctor at the ER said she should rest until Monday. At the same time, there was no way he'd be waiting around his house if their roles were reversed. Besides, he needed this case to be wrapped up by the end of the day so he didn't have to choose between leaving her while she was still in danger and risking his job.

They were on their way to interview Martin Johnson. He managed a pawn shop on the far side of town where he had a reputation for charming the ladies and conning his customers. Blake decided to reserve judgment for the time being. It wouldn't be easy to run a pawn shop, and you'd have to be tough to deal with the people who come back wanting the items they'd pawned when they didn't have the money to pay for them.

"I bought my first gaming system from a pawn shop," Jenny spoke up from the passenger seat of Blake's personal vehicle. "With all of us kids, my parents didn't have the money to buy everyone things like that. I saved up my allowance and money I made from babysitting and bought my first Game Boy and a Mario game from a little pawn shop that isn't even there anymore."

"That's awesome."

"I tell you what, I took good care of that Game Boy. It played like new and cost a fraction of what it would have otherwise. I still have it somewhere."

"I'll bet your siblings were jealous."

She chuckled. "I may or may not have let them play it on occasion in exchange for doing some of my chores."

That made Blake laugh. "I'll bet you were the peace-keeper in your family, weren't you?"

He pictured her as a happy kid with her hair in pigtails and an infectious smile. He'd be willing to bet she'd had all kinds of friends.

That seemed to surprise her. She looked at him, an eyebrow raised. "How'd you know that?"

"It was just a guess, but I based it on how you try to put everyone at ease. You're great with adults and kids alike. Everyone seems to be comfortable with you. I bet you were the kid in school that other kids would confide in."

Jenny shrugged. Even though she didn't respond, he knew he was right.

The GPS announced that they were getting close to their destination. It wasn't the best part of town, and most of the stores had bars over their windows and doors.

"There it is." Jenny pointed out a sign that read *Treasure Trove Pawn Shop* painted boldly on the front of the store.

Blake parked in front of the store. They got out of the car together, and Jenny pulled on the top of her uniform to straighten it. She'd changed before they headed out because she wanted it to be clear she was questioning Johnson in an official capacity.

He'd followed suit, changing into a pair of khakis and a button-down shirt.

Both had put on a bulletproof vest beneath their shirts. After three attempts, they weren't taking any chances.

He pulled the door open for Jenny, and a bell chimed to announce their arrival.

"Come on in. Let me know if you're looking for anything in particular."

The disembodied voice came from the back of the store. There was no one manning the cash register at the small counter ahead.

Jenny raised her voice. "We're looking for Martin Johnson. I believe he manages the store."

A tall, heavy-set man rounded the corner with a charming smile on his face that faded the moment he saw her uniform. A hint of a scowl appeared momentarily before all emotion disappeared completely. He stuck his hands in the pockets of his worn jeans and leaned against the counter.

"What can I do for you, officer?" His words were a direct contrast to his mannerisms.

Johnson might be annoyed that they were there, but if he recognized Jenny, he hid it well.

"I'm Officer Durant, and this is Agent Patterson. I'm sure you've heard about the bombing at the courthouse the other day. There was another attempted bombing at a residence last night. You wouldn't happen to know anything about either of them, would you?"

"If you're accusing me, I run a pawn shop by day, and I'm a janitor at the mall at night. Both locations have all kinds of video cameras. I guarantee you'll find my alibi there." He didn't even blink as he stared Jenny down.

Blake cleared his throat. "You may not have pulled off this job, but there's a decent chance you know who did. We know you've shown an interest in explosives before."

Johnson barked out a laugh. "You think there's an Explosives Anonymous group out there? Or a club where people gather to discuss ways to blow things up?" He looked at Jenny and jabbed a thumb in Blake's direction. "Where'd you dig this guy up?"

She ignored his question. "There aren't too many people in Destiny with a connection to explosives whose names are in the system. There's someone in town who's responsible for three deaths so far. If you know of anyone who's new to the area, or even if you've heard rumors of someone claiming responsibility, we need you to tell us before more people get hurt."

Blake looked around the store. It might be cluttered, but it was clean. As the manager, that likely fell on Johnson. "It looks like you're doing just fine for yourself. You can't be happy that your name came up in this investigation thanks to cases from years ago. Helping the police now would go a long way toward setting yourself up as an asset instead of a possible suspect."

Johnson broke eye contact for the first time and pushed away from the counter. He glanced at the front door. "Look, I may not have a glamorous job, but I've been on the straight and narrow for a long time. I've got a kid, and I'm trying to do right by him." He hesitated. "Look for Eddie Bost. Rumor has it he's connected when it comes to locating those hard-to-find materials."

"And where would we find Eddie Bost?" Jenny pulled out her phone and waited for the information.

"He hangs out at the bar on Mimosa Street most evenings." He grinned at them, but there was an underlying nervousness about the way he shifted his position again. It was clear he wasn't happy about passing along the name.

"I appreciate the information." Jenny pulled a card from her pocket. "If you think of anything else, or if new information comes along, I'd appreciate it if you'd let me know."

Johnson used two fingers to take the card from her. "Yep."

They turned and walked out of the pawn shop, the bell on the door announcing their departure. Blake pictured Johnson tearing the card in half and promptly tossing it in the trash.

He waited until they were both in the car before speaking. "What did you think?"

"He didn't seem to recognize me at all, and he seemed genuinely nervous about being associated with the bombing."

"That's the impression I got, too. He seemed genuine when he talked about his kid, didn't he?"

Jenny shrugged. "I read about Johnson's past. His mom was in and out of rehab for drug use, and I don't think he ever even knew his dad. As a kid, he didn't have much of a chance. Maybe he wants to change that for his own son. Break the cycle. If that's the case, I have nothing but respect for what he's trying to do."

"Agreed. It takes courage to do everything you can to not repeat your parents' mistakes." He started the car and pulled away from the curb.

"Sounds like you speak from experience."

He glanced over to find her watching him curiously, her expression open.

Now, it was his turn to shrug. "My parents were great

parents—individually. I have no memories of them getting along with each other. I remember my fifth birthday party. I got to invite two neighbor boys over, and my parents fought the whole time. Sure, they did most of it in whispers, but I noticed, and it was mortifying."

"I'm sure that was terrible. I'm sorry that happened."

"If it tells you anything, I was relieved when they finally got a divorce. I was eight. At least then, the fighting had mostly stopped. They had joint custody, and I spent the rest of my childhood going between the two of them. I mean, it wasn't all bad. They compensated by making sure we spent quality time together. I have a lot of great memories spent with each of them. I still talk to them both regularly. But birthdays and holidays are always split. I'm convinced that, if something happened to me, they'd have two funerals just so they wouldn't have to attend one together."

The truth was, he'd grown up scared he'd also end up marrying someone that he'd later see as his enemy. It'd been traumatic enough that he'd always figured he'd stay single. He was fine with that, too, until he met Jenny.

With one hand on the steering wheel, he rested his other arm on the console.

"Wow, I can't even imagine. I'm sorry that it was like that for you." She folded her hands together and laid them in her lap.

"You know the saying about how the apple doesn't fall far from the tree? It's hard not to worry about that sometimes."

"Is that why you're not married?"

Chapter Twenty-Three

Jenny couldn't believe she'd asked such an intrusive question. Of course she wondered if his parents' relationship had caused him not to want to get married, but that didn't mean she needed to voice it out loud. "I'm sorry. That was way too personal of a question."

Blake glanced at her as he pulled into a parking lot. He grabbed a spot at the back, put the car in park, and shifted to face her.

"It's a big reason. I always figured the best way to avoid making the same mistakes was to make sure I wasn't in a similar position."

He looked down at her hands, and she realized she was picking at one of her thumbnails. She stretched her fingers out and placed them, palms down on her legs.

What Blake said made perfect sense. She couldn't imagine growing up in a home where her parents hated each other. For her, it was very much the opposite. Her mom and dad had such a loving relationship that it was quite a standard to live up to.

Blake gently nudged her arm with his elbow. "It was a relatively easy decision because I'd never known a woman who made me consider a serious relationship. Until I met a certain Destiny police officer last year."

His words turned her steady heart rate into a gallop. She raised an eyebrow and gave him an unconvinced look. "You had a funny way of showing it. I was sure you hated working with me."

"Far from it. I was distancing myself."

"It was effective," she said wryly.

"Then, when I took the assignment here and started working with you again, I realized that distancing myself wasn't working anymore." His hazel eyes sparkled. "I was kinda kicking myself for sabotaging things with you originally."

She gave a quiet laugh. "I'm not going to lie. I dreaded working with you again when I heard we'd both been assigned to Grassle's detail."

Blake slapped a hand over the left side of his chest as though she'd wounded his heart. "And now?"

"You're all right, Agent Patterson." She tried to keep a straight face but knew she was probably failing miserably. "I might even go so far as to put you on my list of top three favorite partners."

He tipped his head back and laughed. "Well, I suppose that is high praise." His expression sobered as he regarded her. "When this is all over, I'd like to talk about seeing you outside of any joint assignments. Is that something you might be open to?"

"I'd like that." She still didn't know what that would look like. But one thing she was certain of was that she'd regret it if she didn't at least consider the possibilities.

He held his hand out, and she placed her hand in his.

"Then we need to stop this bomber. Unfortunately, we're going to have to wait a few hours before trying to track down Bost at the bar." He glanced at her. "Are you up to stopping by Malone's place?"

She nodded immediately. She didn't look forward to talking to the guy.

Anyone could change—she'd seen that first-hand—but experience taught her that most men who hit women and held them with such contempt rarely shifted their views. The image of Malone's girlfriend's compound fracture had frequented Jenny's dreams for weeks afterward. She'd never understand how anyone could injure another human being like that.

"I think he's our best bet. Guys like that don't forget the women they think disrespected them. The only thing about Malone is that I can't see him resorting to a bomb. He's more of a hands-on guy." She fought back a shudder. "I think he'd be more likely to pound on my front door and charge his way in for revenge than to try to get it from a distance."

"Six years is a long time, especially behind bars. We should have Logan do a search on his cellmates. See if he spent any time with another prisoner who was known to have experience with explosives."

"That's a good idea. I'll call him on the way to Malone's house."

Blake gave her hand one more squeeze before releasing it and putting Carlton Malone's address into GPS. As he drove, Jenny called Logan and relayed their thoughts about who he might have had contact with while in prison.

"I'll get on that right away," Logan said. "I'll let you know what I find."

"Thanks, Logan."

Her phone pinged, and she looked at the text that came through. It was a picture from her mom—one of Jenny and Blake dancing at the wedding. She hadn't even realized anyone noticed, much less took a picture. It wasn't a bad one, either.

"Everything okay?"

She turned her phone so he could see the picture. "Mom just sent me this."

Blake flashed her a smile. "And it may be my new favorite. Send it to me, will you?"

Jenny saved it to her phone and then sent it to his. A moment later, his phone pinged.

It was silly, but there was something about the picture that made whatever was going on between them seem much more real.

She forced her thoughts back to the case. "It might be a good idea for you to take point when we talk to Malone. He won't want to talk to a woman, anyway. Then we can see if he recognizes me and how he reacts when I'm there listening in on the conversation."

"Sure, that sounds good."

GPS guided them the rest of the way to his house, which turned out to be a large, two-story home nestled right in the middle of one of the more affluent neighborhoods in Destiny.

Interesting.

"I wonder if he's staying with someone or if this place is his," she mused.

"If it's his, I'd like to know how he managed to afford it, considering he hasn't been working for six years."

Jenny called Logan again and put the phone on speaker. "Hey, Logan. We just pulled up to the address we have for

Carlton Malone. This place is huge. Can you tell us who actually owns it?"

"Yep. One moment." They listened to the sounds of computer keys tapping in the background. "The house is in his name. He purchased it for over two million just days after he was released from prison. Want me to dive into his financials?"

"Please."

"Will do. Logan out."

Blake pulled into the circle driveway out front and drove around to park close to the exit. They reported in with their location before getting out of the vehicle and walking to the double front door.

Jenny rang the doorbell, which chimed loudly inside.

A minute later, one half of the door swung open to reveal a woman in her mid-twenties. She wore the kind of dress Jenny would expect to see at a night club complete with sparkles and what looked like a diamond necklace.

She looked back and forth between them, truly puzzled to see them there. "Is something wrong, officer?"

Her voice was so soft and feminine, Jenny wondered if it was really like that or if she forced it to sound so mousey.

"We're looking for Carlton Malone. We need to speak with him for a few minutes. Is he available?"

Her baby blue eyes widened slightly as she nodded. "I'll let him know. Please wait here."

With that, the door closed in front of them.

Jenny exchanged looks with Blake. The house had a doorbell camera, so they refrained from making any comments.

How was it that a man who served six years in prison for beating his ex-girlfriend, and was released from jail barely a month ago already seemed to have another woman in his life? The idea infuriated Jenny.

It wasn't simply that he'd gone from jail to apparently living the high life but that this woman was willing to put herself in a dangerous position by being there at all.

She tried to set her negative views aside as they waited patiently until the doorknob finally jiggled five minutes later.

When it opened again, Malone stood in the doorway. Jenny wasn't especially well versed in high-end men's clothing, but she'd be willing to bet he spent more on those shoes, pants, and jacket than she made in a month.

He zeroed in on Jenny immediately, his gaze narrowing and a muscle in his jaw tightening, just moments before he gave them both a wide smile. "Officer Durant. Wonderful to see you again. To what do I owe the pleasure?"

Chapter Twenty-Four

On paper, Blake had disliked Malone immensely. That the man could take out his anger on a woman with a baseball bat infuriated him. Seeing him in person only reinforced his original opinion. The guy was just plain evil.

When Malone first saw Jenny, there was no missing the unadulterated hatred that flashed in his eyes. The man quickly schooled his features, but his continued interest in her, coupled with an added amusement, put Blake on high alert.

"I'm Agent Patterson with the FBI. Nice house. It looks like you've done quite well for yourself here."

Malone spread his arms wide and tilted his head. "When you know how to invest, six years is nothing but an opportunity to build up your nest egg."

That would be quite the trick since there was no way he'd have been able to maintain so much as a savings account while he was behind bars.

Malone quirked an eyebrow as though daring them to

contradict him. "I'd invite you inside, but I just had the floors cleaned."

Blake leaned against one of the pillars, going for nonchalant when he'd prefer to drag the guy back to the precinct for questioning. "That's quite all right. We can speak out here."

Malone shrugged as if it didn't matter to him what they did.

Blake had decided an indirect line of questioning would be the best way to approach Malone. "We're investigating the bombing at the courthouse earlier this week as well as another threat late Saturday. Where were you on Saturday between ten a.m. and six p.m.?"

Where Malone had focused on Jenny when they first arrived, he was now avoiding her completely, which was just fine with Blake.

"That's a long stretch of time there, *agent*. I was a busy man on Saturday. Played golf with some buddies, mowed the backyard, and then my girl and I hung out the rest of the evening. I can give you names, numbers, and locations if you want to verify all of that."

Blake pulled a notebook from his pocket and produced a pen. "That would be great."

Malone plucked them from his hand and went to sit on a large rock in the front yard that was part of the landscaping. As fancy as the house was, the landscaping itself was rather plain. It mostly consisted of large rocks strategically placed in rock beds with a few bushes here and there.

"While you're at it," Blake began, "go ahead and include anyone who might be able to verify your location during the bombing of the courthouse." He gave Malone a specific time frame to account for.

Their suspect lifted his head and pierced Jenny with a

look before turning his attention to Blake. "I thought you had people who were paid to do this kind of work. Sounds like someone's slacking off." He smirked, finished the list, and handed back the paper and pen.

Jenny, who had been giving them some space, walked over to stand right next to Blake. The movement earned her Malone's full attention which included a glare and narrowing of his eyes.

"One last thing," Blake began. "Is there any reason why you'd want to bomb the courthouse or target any of the individuals who had a hand in getting you convicted?"

Malone laughed at that and fixed his gaze on Jenny. "Let me guess. Someone's finally out to get you for meddling in everyone else's business, and it's got your panties all in a twist." He sneered. "Trust me, if I was going to target you, I'd want you to know it was me." He winked. "Now, if you'll excuse me, my lady is waiting for me inside."

With that, he sauntered back to the front door and disappeared inside without another look.

Blake waited for Jenny to get settled in the passenger seat of the car before going around to the driver's side. He started the engine and pulled away from Malone's house.

"He is a ... piece of work." Blake glanced over at Jenny. "Are you okay?"

"Yeah." Her left hand was clenched and resting on her leg. She had the other arm propped up against the window. "Seeing that woman in his house made me so angry. Guys like Malone don't change, and she's going to end up like his other ex. Or worse. Even if she doesn't realize who he is or what he's done, he's not exactly suave. How does he keep getting women to trust him like they do?"

"It's probably a combination of his money and her desperation. Something tells me he's probably a high spender when his lady of the week acts devoted." He couldn't keep the sarcasm from his voice. "I don't understand it either, Jenny. If I found out a sister or friend was seeing a guy like that..."

"I know. I wish we could do more to prevent repeat offenses." She released a heavy sigh, followed by several moments of silence before speaking again. "I don't think he's responsible, though. He's not wrong. If he decided to get back at me, he'd beat me to a pulp with his fists, not set up some elaborate explosion and hope I'm the one who gets killed. He'd want me to know it was him."

Blake didn't like the thought of that, but he had gotten the same impression, which felt like a double loss. It would've been nice to catch the man after Jenny and lock Malone up again all in one arrest.

Her phone rang, and she tapped the speaker button. "Hey, Logan. Agent Patterson and I are both here. We've got you on speaker."

"So I took a look at Malone's financials. He inherited a large sum of money from his father when he died about fifteen years ago. We're talking two million dollars. He took that and invested it in a variety of commodities, crypto currency, real estate, and more. Then, he put the rest in a savings account. By diversifying his wealth, he managed to nearly double his worth over the course of the following five years."

"What happened to that money once he was convicted?"

"He lost quite a bit to court fees, medical bills for the woman he assaulted, plus pain and suffering. What was left, which was no small amount, he signed over to a woman by the name of Kiki Devereux to be used in raising their son."

Blake looked at Jenny, and she seemed just as surprised as he was. "Do you have a picture of Ms. Devereux?"

"One sec, I'll text it to you both."

Blake pulled into a parking lot, put his car in park, and took his phone out of his pocket. When the text arrived, he showed the picture to Jenny.

"It's the woman who answered the door," she confirmed.

"Which means he has control of all that money again. Whether by mutual agreement or manipulation is anyone's guess." Though if Blake were a betting man, he'd go with the latter.

Jenny shifted in her seat. "Hey, Logan, are you at the station?"

"Yep. There's a bunch of people here. Someone brought in sandwiches, and the chief said he's having dinner delivered later."

"Good to know. Thanks, Logan."

"You bet."

Jenny ended the call and tapped the phone several times against her knee. When she finally raised her chin, she looked sad. "I can't just sit around at the house. Waiting for news. Waiting for you to leave."

"I know. Me either. Let's drive back to your place. I'll grab my stuff, and we'll take both vehicles back over to the station. Hang out there the rest of the day. It'll make it easier when I have to leave. Lots of distractions."

"Yeah."

He reached for her hand and laced their fingers together with a squeeze.

It didn't matter how many distractions there were. Walking away from Jenny tonight, especially if the case was still open, wasn't going to be easy.

Chapter Twenty-Five

Once they got back to her house, Jenny thought she and Blake might have a chance to talk. It didn't work out that way. She was on the phone with her mom while he packed up his things, and then his boss called while she gathered what she thought she might need for the rest of the day. Before she hung up with her mom, Nate called for an update. She told him about their conversations with Malone and Johnson, as well as the man that Johnson said may be connected to explosive materials.

It wasn't until they were on her front porch, and she was locking the door, that they were both finally off the phone. She slipped her keys into her pocket and suppressed a sigh.

He didn't hesitate to step close and put an arm around her waist.

"When I get back to my office, I'm going to send you the days that I have off from work. We're going to get our schedules coordinated. Then I'm driving to Destiny to take you out on a proper first date." He brushed some hair off her forehead and gently touched the healing spot on her ear. "Deal?"

"Deal."

He tugged her close and lowered his mouth to hers. She melted into him, thankful for his strong arm holding her up, so she didn't melt into a puddle at his feet. With one hand, she threaded her fingers through the hair at the base of his neck.

Blake kissed her until she could hardly think. When he leaned back, he groaned and then buried his face in her hair.

"Sweetheart, we'd better get going, or I'm going to kiss you like that until my boss drags me away."

She laughed at the thought. "I'm not seeing the problem."

He cupped her face with both of his hands. "We're going to figure out a way to make this work."

Jenny nodded. "I know."

He gave her one last kiss that was brief but oh, so sweet.

Fifteen minutes later, they pulled into the precinct parking lot and went inside. They both stored their things at Jenny's desk and joined the others in a conference room. Nate immediately motioned her over.

"These two men work for Angelo Sandoval. We suspect he hires them to take care of problem customers, but that has yet to be proven. Do you recognize either of them? Seen them wandering around your neighborhood or anything like that?"

She took her time looking at each of the photos. "I've never seen them before."

"How about this man? His name is Eddie Bost, and he's the guy that Martin Johnson told you and Patterson about."

"The explosives guy?" She looked at the picture and frowned. "Nope."

Nate quickly covered his disappointment. "That's okay. We're going to go down to the bar in a few hours. From what Logan could dig up on him, he's more likely to supply materials used in explosives than he is to actually set them himself."

"I hope it leads to something."

Jenny truly wished she'd seen one of them. They needed a break in this case—any break.

Someone touched her shoulder, and she turned to find Blake handing her a plate. He'd gotten her a turkey and cheddar sandwich and barbecue chips. The fact that he remembered warmed her heart. "Thank you."

"You're welcome. Make sure you take the time to eat, okay?"

"I will."

The afternoon and evening were grueling. Every time they got a possible lead in the case, they'd wind up at a dead end. It was frustrating to Blake, but what he hated most was seeing Jenny so discouraged. It didn't help that there was this silent clock counting down the time he had left to be there to support and protect her.

Earlier in the evening, Nate had sent a patrol to the bar Eddie Bost was supposed to frequent with instructions to let the precinct know when he was spotted. It was nearly seven before that call finally came through.

"Patterson, you're with me." Nate stood and reached for his jacket. He turned to Jenny. "Hang in there. We'll be back soon."

She nodded and mouthed, "Be careful," to Blake as he followed Nate out.

They got into Nate's unmarked car and headed to the bar across town. Blake prayed this would lead to some helpful information.

Nate glanced over at him. "So, you and Jenny, huh?" There was no humor or judgment there, only a statement.

"I hope so. There's still a lot to figure out."

"I get that. Probably more than you realize. I speak from experience when I say that. If it's meant to be, things will work out eventually."

"She's worth the wait."

"That she is." Nate gave a nod of approval. "All right, Bost is an interesting character in that he tends to deal in hard-to-find items. He technically doesn't break any laws because everything he sells is legal for other uses. But he has the connections. Plus, most people pay him in cash, so there's no record."

"Which comes in handy if you're trying to get materials to build a bomb and don't want your purchases being traced to the local hardware store."

"Exactly. Bost hasn't popped up on our radar in a while, but for Johnson to mention him and for him to show up at the bar, I figure he's probably been operating under the radar all this time."

Nate waited for the streetlight to turn green and pressed on the gas. As they got close, he spoke into his radio. "Officer Smith, I'm pulling up to the bar now."

"He's still in there."

"Very good. You can return to the station and head out for the night."

"Yes, sir. Thank you."

They parked within sight of the front door and headed in.

Blake spotted Bost. "Back, left corner."

"I see him."

They threaded their way through the crowd of customers and approached Bost's corner booth. A second man was sitting with him who stood quickly and excused himself.

Bost, a heavy-set man in his fifties with a ridiculous comb-over, leaned forward and placed his folded hands on the table. His expression gave nothing away. "What can I do for you, gentlemen?"

Nate held out his badge. "Eddie Bost? I'm Detective Nate Walker, and this is FBI Agent Blake Patterson. We'd like to ask you a few questions."

Bost motioned to the large booth. "Have a seat." He motioned for a waitress. "What can I get you two?"

Blake held up a hand to tell him he didn't want anything.

"Nothing for me, thank you," Nate said. "I'm sure you've seen the news about the explosion at the courthouse."

"Nasty business, that." Bost took a drink of his beer. "Before this goes any farther, I want to make it clear that none of the goods I sell are stolen, and I discourage my clients from using any supplies in illegal activities."

"Understood." When Bost nodded, Nate continued. "The individual responsible for the courthouse bombing rigged another device that was discovered before it could be detonated. We have reason to believe that may not be the last we see of him. Have you had any customers lately who have expressed an interest in materials that could potentially be used in the construction of explosive devices?"

Bost took another gulp of his beverage. "That's not something I get many calls for. Most people can look online for instructions and buy the supplies necessary from the hardware store." He held up a finger. "But I did have a potential customer contact me earlier this week. Some guy I'd never seen before. Didn't catch his name. He wasn't looking for parts, though. He wanted to hire me to build and provide the complete device. Something I immediately told him I wouldn't do. That's not how I operate."

Blake suspected Bost wasn't telling the whole truth when it came to the source of the goods he sold. However, he believed that he wouldn't build a bomb and simply hand it over to a customer. There was no way that wouldn't be traced back to him.

"Was this individual upset when you refused your services?"

"He seemed surprised and irritated. I wouldn't say he was upset. More like I'd inconvenienced him, if you get what I'm saying. He left shortly after that, and I haven't seen him since. I got the feeling he wasn't from around here."

"Did you speak to him here?"

"Right around this time Monday night."

Nate gave Blake a nod, and Blake scooted out of the booth. He found someone up at the bar and flagged him over. "I need to speak to your manager, please." He pointed to the badge on his belt.

"If you'll wait here, I'll let him know."

The bartender returned in minutes with another man who held out his hand. "Trevor Gates. Can I help you?"

Blake introduced himself and shook the man's hand. "Do you have security footage from Monday evening available?" He tilted his head toward one of the many cameras in the room.

"We should. Our videos are stored on the cloud and are kept for a month before they're deleted to make room."

"I'm going to need a copy of your footage from Monday, let's say going around five to ten p.m."

"I can do that, but it'll take a few minutes. The files are rather large. I'm not sure how to get them to you."

"Not a problem. Let me put you in touch with the police department's IT guy. He'll walk you through it."

Blake used the bar's phone to call Logan, told him the situation, and then passed the phone over to Trevor. Once they were talking, he walked back to the table and sat down again. "There's security footage. The manager is going to get the files over to Logan."

"Excellent." Nate turned to Bost. "Can you give us a description of the man you spoke with?"

"Like I said, it was about this time on Monday night, right here at this booth. White guy with silver hair and a baseball cap. Tall, super thin. Honestly, kind of sickly looking. Nothing much else to say about him."

"Well, we appreciate the help, Mr. Bost. You have yourself a good night."

"You two as well." He gave them both a nod and reached for his beer.

Blake and Nate went to the back of the bar to wait for the manager to return and let them know the security files had been sent over, then verified with Logan that he'd received them. Blake hoped and prayed that this, finally, would be the lead they were looking for.

Chapter Twenty-Six

I t was a huge relief when Blake and Nate made it back to the precinct at half past nine and even more so when they relayed what had happened at the bar. Now it was after ten, and Jenny sat with the two of them, Clint Baker, and Logan at a table in the conference room.

Logan had the security footage up on his computer and was going through it now, looking for the person that Bost described.

For the first time in the last few days, Jenny had hope that this was going to lead to some answers.

Clint had brought the pizza from earlier out of the fridge and was eating a cold slice of pepperoni. Jenny finally reached for a slice. She wasn't necessarily hungry, but she was nervous and needed something to take her mind off the waiting.

She slid the pizza box over to Blake. "Want some?"

"I'm not a fan of cold pizza. Thanks, though." He glanced at his watch.

It was a reminder that he was going to need to head out

soon. She pushed that thought into the back of her mind, too.

"It was practically a staple at my house," Jenny told him. "My parents would make or buy way more pizza than we could eat—and that was a lot. Then we all looked forward to eating it for breakfast the next day."

Blake shook his head as he made an exaggerated look of disgust.

Clint held up his second slice. "Hey, don't knock it till you've tried it."

"I'm good. More for you guys." Blake gave her a wink.

Logan cleared his throat. "Okay, I think I've got him."

He turned on the large TV against one wall and shared his screen. "Here's the corner booth, and that's Bost sitting there. Our person of interest is walking in... now."

They all watched as a wiry man in a baseball cap approached Bost and joined him at the table. The conversation was a short one, and it was clear that Bost dismissed his potential client. Judging from the way the second man stood quickly and strode away, he wasn't happy with Bost's answer.

Logan backed up the video and paused at the best view of their suspect's face. It wasn't at all clear enough to run facial recognition.

Nate frowned. "Do you think you can clean that up, Logan?"

"This isn't a lot to work with, but I can give it a try. It'll take the software much of the night to run. As soon as I have an image, I'll run it through facial recognition. See if it matches anyone in the system."

"That'll be great." Nate took in a deep breath and stood. "I think that's about all we're going to accomplish tonight.

You should all go home and get some rest. Tomorrow will be here before we know it."

Jenny stood as well but avoided looking at Blake. If everyone was leaving, that meant he would be heading back to Austin. He had an hour and a half drive before he could get some sleep. At least it'd be a short night for him.

Clint shoved the last bite of pizza in his mouth and closed the box. There was still half a pizza inside. He shoved it across the table for Nate and swallowed his mouthful. "You should take it for Bailey and the boys."

"Thanks." He turned to Jenny. "I'm going to follow you back to your place to make sure you get in okay. There's an officer out front and will be all night along with another regular patrol."

"Thank you. I'm sure I'll be fine."

Clint bid them all good night and took his leave. Logan packed up his computer and did the same, stopping to shake Blake's hand on the way out. "I look forward to working with you again."

"You, too," Blake returned.

Nate extended a hand. "We appreciate your assistance, Blake. It's been good to get to know you. Don't be a stranger."

Blake gave it a firm shake. "I won't. Same goes for you."

Nate gently squeezed Jenny's arm. "I'll meet you guys out back in a few minutes."

Jenny waited for Nate to leave the room before turning to face Blake. "With any luck, Logan will be able to clean that image up, get a hit with facial recognition, and we'll have him in custody by lunch tomorrow."

"I hope so. I wish I could stay until then. I don't like the idea of you being at your house alone tonight." He glanced at the door to the conference room and stepped closer to her. "If you're worried about anything, put in a call to the officer outside. Don't risk it."

"Promise. And I need you to text me when you get home regardless of the time. Are you sure you're not too tired to drive?"

"I'll be fine. I'll stop along the way if I need to. And yes, I'll text you when I get home." He smiled then, and the affection in his gaze warmed her heart. "I'm going to miss you, Durant."

"I'm going to miss you, too, Patterson." Her voice caught despite her intention to keep her emotions at bay. She placed a hand against his chest and focused on the feel of his heartbeat against her palm.

He covered her hand with his own and leaned in for a kiss that was as full of promises as it was sweet. Tears pricked the back of her eyelids, which was just ridiculous. A week ago, she'd found him annoying and rude. Now she wished he didn't have to leave at all.

The kiss ended way before she wanted it to, but she was also aware of the possibility that someone might come back into the conference room.

Before he let go of her hand, he started to pray. "Heavenly Father, we ask for guidance as everyone works tirelessly to solve this case. I also pray that You protect Jenny and keep her safe from anyone who might try to harm her."

She nodded, her eyes closed. "Please help Blake get back to Austin safely. Guide him as he dives into a new assignment tomorrow."

He squeezed her hand. "Thank You for bringing us together. Give us wisdom going forward. Amen."

"Amen." She swallowed her emotions and blinked the tears away. "Come on, we'd better get our stuff and get out of here."

A few minutes later, they met Nate at the back door leading to the rear parking lot where all three of them had parked.

"Be safe going home, Blake."

"Will do. Give my best to Bailey and the boys." The men shook hands again.

Blake gave Jenny's hand a squeeze. "I'll let you know when I get home. Get some rest and update me on the case tomorrow."

"I will."

When he released her hand, she tucked it into her pocket and blinked away another round of tears that threatened to spill over.

Nate made sure the door was locked and led the way to their cars. He followed her all the way home, where she waved at an officer parked in front of her house. Nate insisted on going in with her to clear the house then bid her good night.

Jenny locked the door behind him and leaned against it as she looked around the living room. The house was way too quiet now. She kicked off her shoes, sat down on the couch, and pulled the blanket onto her lap. That's where she dozed until an hour and a half later when Blake texted her to let her know he'd gotten home safely.

> I'm glad. Get some rest tonight. Thanks again for everything.

> You sleep well, too. I'll talk to you tomorrow.

> Okay. Good night.

> Good night, sweetheart.

Only then did Jenny finally change into some pajamas and, after several nights sleeping in the recliner, climbed into her own bed.

The last thing that went through her mind before she fell asleep was a prayer asking God to keep them both safe.

Chapter Twenty-Seven

Monday morning, Jenny couldn't stop yawning. She'd gone to sleep late, and then she woke up several times to a house that was much too quiet. It was four in the morning before she finally fell into a deep sleep, only for her alarm to wake her up two and a half hours later.

The first thing she did was text Blake a "good morning" before jumping in the shower and getting ready for the day. She grabbed a granola bar from the pantry, decided to wait for the coffee at work, and headed out. With a wave of thanks to the officer sitting out front, she made her way to the precinct.

As she pulled into the parking lot, a ping announced an incoming text.

> Good morning! I'm praying you guys identify the bomber today. Keep me updated.

> I will. Good luck with your new assignment.

Thanks. I should find out more this
morning. Talk to you soon.

She smiled to herself and went inside. There was barely enough time to get a cup of coffee before Logan found her.

"Hey, there you are. I was able to clear up that picture enough to see the guy's features. I was just about to take it to Walker if you want to look at it, too."

"Absolutely. Let's go." She took a sip of her coffee and nearly groaned at how good it was.

That was exactly what she needed to jump-start the day. If Tia ever decided to leave the precinct, they would have to corner her and demand to know where she got the coffee. There was no way they could go back to generic coffee after this.

She noticed Logan laughing at her. "Hey, it's what gets me moving in the morning. Do you not drink coffee?"

"Can't stand the stuff. It smells good—I'd get an air freshener that smells just like that in a heartbeat."

"Have you tried the coffee here? It's on a whole different level."

Logan knocked on the door leading to Nate's office.

"I did, and I think it offended Tia when I couldn't finish it."

She chuckled.

"Come in," Nate called to them. He looked up when they opened the door and zeroed in on Logan. "You got something?"

"Yep, I've got good news and bad news." He plopped down in one of the chairs and opened his laptop. "The good news is, I was able to clean up that image of our suspect. The bad news is, there was no match with facial recognition software."

He pulled the picture up and turned it around so Nate and Jenny could see it.

Jenny examined the photo, hoping that she'd recognize the man. Disappointment hit hard when she realized she'd never seen him before and neither had Nate.

"Then we're back to where we started." It took Jenny some effort to keep the discouragement from her voice. "Do you mind if I send this to Blake, just in case?"

"That's a good idea," Nate agreed.

"I'm sending a copy to your phone now." Logan typed something out on his computer and hit enter with a flourish. "And done."

Her phone pinged with the incoming text. She saved the photo and then sent it to Blake with a short message asking him to let her know if he'd seen the guy before.

"So, what's next?"

Nate reached for his cup of coffee and took a sip. "If we go on the assumption that this man is our bomber, and he couldn't buy what he wanted from Bost, then it stands to reason that he had to make the device himself. Logan, I want you to get with the lab for a list of components and see where those might have been purchased here in Destiny. Once we have that list, we'll go to every store, show this picture, and see if anyone recognizes him. Maybe we'll get lucky."

Blake was starting his Monday out tired. Once he'd gotten home and let Jenny know he'd arrived safely, he'd had no problem going to sleep. Unfortunately, nightmares had awakened him at least twice. He was thankful he couldn't remember the details in his dreams, but he did know they had something to do with Jenny being in trouble and him not being able to get there in time to help. He'd finally awakened for the day at just after five, frustrated and missing Jenny.

At least it gave him time to get a load of laundry done and his duffel bag packed with fresh clothing.

It was weird being back at the office in Austin again. Blake had only been in Destiny a week, but it seemed much longer. For one thing, the difference in rush hour traffic between the two was substantial. He missed the ease of getting around a smaller town.

He filled a to-go cup with coffee in the agency break room, slapped on a lid, and took a sip.

He also missed Tia's coffee.

Friend and fellow FBI agent, Lewis Zimmerman, nudged him out of the way and got himself his own coffee. He glanced over and frowned. "What's the scowl for?" He didn't wait for an answer before taking a gulp of his hot drink.

"It was a long night. I didn't get in until late."

Lewis lifted his cup. "Thank goodness for caffeine."

"Yep." Blake took another sip and hoped the effects would kick in soon. "Have you seen Torrance yet?"

Their SSA—or Supervisory Special Agent—was the one who insisted that Blake return from his assignment in Destiny. It meant that he had another assignment waiting, and Blake was ready to get started. At least it would keep his mind busy.

"He's been on the phone in his office since I arrived." Lewis raised an eyebrow. "I heard you were hoping to stay in Destiny longer. Sounded like your case didn't go the way it was expected to."

"It sure didn't." He told Lewis a little about the situation. "The woman I initially went down there to protect should be giving her statement today and will hopefully enter WITSEC without a problem. It's leaving Officer Durant there when they still don't know who's after her that's bothering me."

As though she somehow knew that he was talking about her, a text came through with a photo attached. Apparently, Logan had been able to clean up the image from the bar's security tapes.

He zoomed in on the photo and frowned. The man looked vaguely familiar, but Blake couldn't quite place where he'd seen him. "Sorry, Lewis, I need to make a quick call."

Lewis took another drink of his coffee and headed back to his office.

Blake dialed Jenny's number.

"Hey, you."

Just the sound of her voice brightened his mood substantially. He wished he had time to visit for a few minutes, but his boss stuck his head out of his office and waved for Blake to come in.

"Hey, it's good to hear your voice. I'm sorry, I only have a minute. I got that picture, and the guy seems familiar. I can't, for the life of me, figure out where I've seen him before, though. Maybe it was in passing somewhere? It's driving me crazy. If I remember more, I'll call you right away."

"Sounds good. Thanks for letting me know."

"Of course. Be careful, okay?"

"I will. You, too."

They ended the call, and he pocketed his phone before heading over to Ian Torrance's office. He knocked on the doorframe as he walked in. "You wanted to see me?"

"Hey, Blake. Welcome back. I'm sorry to pull you in like this. I know you were wanting to see the other case through."

Blake was frustrated, but he also understood the position his boss was in since they were down two agents already. Torrance normally accepted input and requests from those on his team. If he'd insisted that Blake return to their field office, then there must be a good reason.

"I'm still worried about my PD partner there in Destiny, but they're going to keep me updated as the case progresses. What have we got?"

He listened as Torrance told him about a case in Caldwell that needed FBI collaboration. Blake made notes and truly gave the details of the case his attention. He'd be heading for Caldwell this afternoon, which would put him an hour farther away from Jenny. He tried to ignore the unease that was building like pressure in his chest.

Chapter Twenty-Eight

J enny answered her phone and ducked into one of the small conference rooms for privacy. The station had been busy all morning, and she knew it would be difficult to hear in the bullpen. "How's your day going so far?"

She hadn't expected to hear from Blake again until the end of the day.

"It's been busy. I'm prepping for my new assignment. I'll be leaving this afternoon for Caldwell."

"Any idea how long you'll be there?"

"With any luck, it'll just be a few days. I'll know more once I talk to local law enforcement."

It wasn't like she was going to get to see him anyway, but the idea that he'd be even farther away made her sad. "I hope it goes smoothly. Hey, you called at the perfect time. I just got word that our witness was able to give her testimony, and everything is moving forward as planned."

"That's great. I'm really glad to hear that. Especially after all the hiccups." There were shuffling noises in the background. "Any news on the other front?"

"We've got officers showing the suspect's picture anywhere in town where materials might have been purchased to make the bombs. We're hoping someone will recognize his face and give us a lead. For now, everything has been quiet." She looked at the clock.

It was nearly noon.

"I'm supposed to meet my sister for lunch in half an hour before she and her family drive back to Oklahoma this afternoon. She wants to talk about something important and refuses to wait, but we're meeting at the sandwich place just down the street."

"I wish I were there to watch your back."

"Me, too. Nate's planning to get lunch from there, too, and we'll go at the same time."

"Good. That makes me feel better. I'll be praying someone recognizes the picture, and that'll lead to an ID." He groaned. "I'd better go. Call me if you need me, Jenny. Anytime. Okay?"

"I will. Thanks for checking in. I'll let you know if we get any leads. Good luck in Caldwell—drive safely."

They said goodbye, and she hung up.

It was easy to stay busy for the next half hour until Nate let her know that he was ready to head out to lunch. They decided to take separate vehicles just in case one of them got called out for something.

Her sister, Lisa, was already inside waiting at a table and waved Jenny over. "There you are. I don't know about you, but I'm starving." She tapped a sign that was attached to a stand. "I'm getting the special. I can't remember the last time I had a good chicken salad sandwich."

The picture looked delicious. She loved it when they put both tiny apple pieces and grapes in chicken salad. "I think I'll have the same."

"Yay. That makes it easy. My treat. Iced tea?"

"I'll take a Coke today. Thanks, Lisa."

"No problem. I'll be right back."

Lisa returned a few minutes later with their drinks and a number to set on their table. She didn't waste any time diving into what she wanted to talk about.

"Mom and Dad's fiftieth anniversary is in May, and I thought maybe we could all pool our money and do something really special for them. Like send them on a cruise or maybe to Hawaii. Something that they'd never pay for themselves and would remember forever. What do you think?" Lisa clasped her hands together and laid them on the table as she watched Jenny expectantly.

It wasn't a bad idea. Their parents had worked hard to provide for their kids, and for most of Jenny's childhood, they rarely had the extra money to go on a family vacation, at least not to anywhere fancy like Disneyland or something like that. But they went on adventures in the woods or to the beach. Memorable things that Jenny looked back on fondly.

Maybe it was time that they got to go do something fancy. They deserved it, even if they probably wouldn't arrange something like that themselves. "They'll never agree to it."

"They will if we go through a travel agent and get everything set up. Let them choose a time that works for them, but then tell them it's non-refundable. Guilt alone should make them agree to go." Lisa hiked an eyebrow, a smile on her face.

Jenny laughed. "That's so messed up. Maybe spend the extra money to let them change the dates just in case. You know, cover our bases."

Lisa straightened. "Then you're in?"

"I'm in. Let's see if we can convince the guys."

"Leave it to me. Oh! Here's our food."

Jenny moved her drink over enough to give plenty of room for the basket holding her sandwich, dill pickle, and hand-cut chips. Next time Blake was in town, she'd have to bring him here.

The ease with which he slipped into her thoughts surprised her, and she missed him all over again. She took a bite of her sandwich and pointed to it, giving it a thumbs up.

Lisa wiped her mouth with her napkin. "No kidding. Best chicken salad I've ever had." She popped a chip in her mouth. When she'd swallowed, she leveled Jenny with a serious look. "How are things going with the FBI guy?"

Jenny nearly choked on her sandwich and washed it down with a drink. "Blake had to go back to Austin last night. Now he's headed to Caldwell on another assignment." She tried to keep the conversation casual, but from the way Lisa's gaze narrowed, she wasn't so sure she succeeded.

"Come on, I know you better than that. I saw the way you looked at him. Not to mention the way he watched you. There's definitely something going on between you two."

"It didn't start out that way, but now..." Her face grew hot, and she took another bite of her sandwich. A glance at Nate on the other side of the restaurant reassured her that he was busy with his own meal. At least he couldn't hear their conversation.

"Come on, Jenny. If you can't talk to your sister about these things, then who can you talk to?"

Jenny wasn't sure she wanted to talk to anyone yet. "I really like him." She shrugged. "And the feeling seems to be mutual. But we just started to figure it out on Saturday, and then he had to leave Sunday night. It's all new and confusing. And long distance. Which, given our jobs, isn't going to be something we can easily change."

Lisa looked sad for a moment before she brightened up again. "Where there's a will, there's a way. Besides, if you're meant to be together, things will work out. They always do."

"Really?" Jenny wasn't so sure about that.

Her sister picked up the other half of her sandwich and leaned forward as though she were sharing a great secret. "*Always.*" She grinned. "The two of you look good together. And can you imagine how happy Mom and Dad will be? Maybe you guys can get engaged and tell them on their anniversary, too. They'll be so happy about that they wouldn't dare turn down our gift."

The thought of marrying Blake made the back of her neck heat. She picked up her drink and cupped it with both hands. "Jumping the gun a little there, don't you think?"

It was a good thing Blake wasn't there to hear the conversation. Would it freak him out? Because it didn't freak her out nearly as much as it probably should.

Chapter Twenty-Nine

Now that Blake had everything set at the office, he planned to head out to Caldwell in the next hour or two. After not getting much sleep last night, he really needed to get to bed at a decent time tonight in order to start this new assignment on the right foot.

Right now, he was in Lewis's office sampling some of the teriyaki jerky he'd made. He was forever trying different seasonings and getting Blake's opinion on them.

Blake didn't mind a bit.

Lewis popped a piece in his mouth and chewed thoughtfully. "You know, most people are glad when they put an assignment behind them. At least, you usually are. It's the cop, isn't it?"

Blake covered his surprise with a cough. He gave his friend a dubious look, but Lewis wasn't going to let it go.

"Jenny Durant."

Lewis's eyebrows disappeared beneath the shaggy hair hanging down over his forehead. "I thought she hated you. Obviously, that's changed."

Blake chuckled. "Apparently."

"Good for you, man. Trust me, there's nothing better than knowing you've got a good woman who'll be there no matter what." Lewis ought to know. He was happily married with two kids and another on the way.

"Except for the small problem where she's working in Destiny, and I work here. When I'm not assigned to work somewhere else, that is. We haven't quite figured it out yet. There hasn't been time." Whenever he let his mind go there, he couldn't see a workable solution. At least not an easy one.

"You will. You just have to trust the process."

Blake sure hoped he was right.

He stood, about to excuse himself and head home when his phone rang. *Unknown* popped up on his screen, which wasn't something he saw often. "Hold on a second," he told his friend as he answered the call. "This is Blake Patterson."

"I know." The man on the other side of the phone laughed dryly. "Where do you think you're going?"

Blake put his fingers to his lips to signal for Lewis to stay silent, and then put the phone on speaker.

"I don't know what you're talking about."

"It must be pretty important to leave your little girl-friend while she's still being hunted like an animal."

Blake motioned for Lewis to get someone to trace the call. The other agent nodded and hurried from the room.

There was no doubt in his mind that this was the guy who'd tried to kill Jenny. Anger had his pulse pounding in his ears and his stomach clenching.

Lewis returned with Torrance in tow and Patricia, their tech guru, on a video call on his phone. He propped the phone against a book on his desk.

"What do you want?"

The man on the phone laughed again. "You'll find out soon enough."

The call ended, and Patricia shook her head as she typed furiously on her computer. "I can tell the phone call originated in Destiny, but I wasn't able to get a specific location. He's using a burner phone, which makes it difficult to trace. The next time he calls, I'll continue to analyze the signals from cell towers and see if I can triangulate his position. There's no guarantee he'll stay there, though."

Torrance studied Blake. "Did you recognize the voice?"

"No. Maybe." Right now, he wasn't sure of anything. He stared at his phone, willing it to ring again. Instead, a text came through with attachments. He swiped to find someone had taken pictures of him and Jenny outside her home before they headed back to the station on Sunday. There was a close-up photo of Jenny smiling, another of them kissing, and a third of him holding her in his arms.

The man who took these photos had been out there, watching them, and Blake hadn't even noticed. He'd been so wrapped up in Jenny that he'd missed it. Anger surged along with frustration at himself.

Lewis whistled. "You weren't kidding when you said the assignment got complicated."

Blake went back to the image of Jenny and turned it around to show Torrance. "This was my partner while I was working with the Destiny Police Department, and whoever is after her isn't finished."

Patricia nodded toward his phone. "Send them to me, and I'll pull them up on a bigger screen."

The last thing he wanted was for his new relationship with Jenny to be broadcast among his co-workers, but her life was more important. He sent the pictures to Patricia and ignored the heat climbing up his neck and into his ears.

She must have opened them on her computer screen. "They're high-quality photos. Unless the guy was standing nearby, there's no way he would've gotten images like this from a cell phone zoomed in. He had to be using a DSLR with a decent telephoto lens."

His phone came to life again with another call from the same unknown number. Patricia set something up on her computer and then nodded at Blake to answer the call. He did, immediately putting it on speaker.

The man from earlier spoke. "Have I gotten your attention now?"

"I'm going to ask you again: what do you want?"

"Because of you, I lost everything. Everything! I want you to suffer like I did. I want you to watch someone you care about die right in front of you. But since you left her to fend for herself, I guess I'll have to settle for you knowing she's going to die, and there's nothing you can do to stop it."

A chill washed over Blake. This didn't have anything to do with Jenny's past cases. It had everything to do with *him*. He'd brought this on her when he went to Destiny, and now she was the one who was going to suffer the consequences.

"Whoever you are and whatever I've done to make you angry, this is between us. There's no need to harm anyone else."

The caller laughed. "I put a bomb in her car days ago. I've just been waiting for the right moment to activate it. This seems like as good of a time as any."

With that, the call ended again.

Patricia shook her head. "I've got his location down to a ten-block radius. I'm not sure how much help that's going to be. It looks like he's powered the phone down."

Blake barely heard her as he dialed Jenny's phone number. He had to warn her not to get into her car. The phone rang and rang until finally her voicemail picked up. "Jenny, it's Blake. Do *not* get in your car. There's a bomb." He hung up immediately, texted her the same message, and then called Nate. With any luck, they were still eating lunch and hadn't finished it yet.

"This is Walker. Miss us already, Patterson?"

Blake stared at the image of Jenny's face still up on Patricia's screen.

"Nate, is Jenny still there with you?"

"She just said goodbye to her sister. She grabbed a drink refill, and we're heading out and back to the office now."

Blake braced a hand against Lewis's desk. "There's a bomb in her car. I repeat, there's a bomb in Jenny's car."

In the background, he heard Nate call out, "Jenny! Don't open it! Everyone back away. There's a bomb! Jenny—"

A deafening sound cut Nate off and had Blake jerking the phone away from his ear with a flinch. When he put it back, all he could hear were people screaming before the line went dead.

Chapter Thirty

After hearing Nate's warning, Jenny's hand jerked away from the car, and she automatically ducked down. She waved people away from the vehicle as she started to run across the street. "Go, go! Get away!"

She'd nearly made it to the center of the two-lane road when the car exploded behind her, the sound filling the air as a wave of heat slammed against her back. She dove to the pavement and covered her head.

The sounds of people yelling and shoes hitting the pavement as people ran were the first things Jenny registered. She pushed herself off the ground and ignored the twinge from her already-bruised knee. "Nate?" When she spun around and saw him running toward her, she nearly fell back to the ground in relief. "Thank God."

He reached for her arm. "You okay?"

"Yeah. Yeah, I'm fine." She scanned the crowd of onlookers. "Was anyone hurt?"

"No."

Her car was a ball of flames and dark smoke, and both the car in front of it and Nate's behind it were entirely too close for comfort. Thank goodness Lisa had left minutes before and hadn't been anywhere near the blast.

"How did you know there was a bomb?"

"Blake." Nate pointed at her bag. "Call him and let him know." He pulled his own phone out while he continued to wave people back.

Police cars were already showing up as Jenny saw that she'd missed a call from Blake and called him back. It barely rang once when he answered.

"Jenny?" Blake's voice was clipped. Urgent.

"I'm here. Blake, I'm okay."

"Praise God!" He released a huge breath. "That was the longest few minutes of my life. It sounded like the bomb went off. What about Nate? Anyone else caught in the blast?"

"No one, thanks to you. Nate warned me in the nick of time and backed everyone off before it detonated."

"Jenny, listen. The bomber contacted me, and he claims he could trigger the detonator whenever he wanted to. If that's true, and he was waiting for the right timing, then it means he's close by to see if he succeeded. He's shot at you before, Jenny. You need to get out of there."

"We know what he looks like. If he's here, and if I can spot him, then maybe we can end this right now."

"I *hate* that I'm not there watching your back. Okay, you're going to be looking for someone who appears agitated or angry. He tried to kill you, and he failed. He's not going to be happy about that."

The hair stood on the back of her neck as she scanned both sides of the street. "There are a lot of people. Most are watching the fire department put out what's left of my car."

"This guy isn't going to be watching the fire. He's going

to be focused on you. Take your time and look around. Do you see anyone that stands out?"

She took in a deep breath and then another. Her heart rate lowered, and the adrenaline from earlier ebbed a little. Slowly, she scanned the crowd again. Nate was speaking with officers and probably assigning them to take statements from witnesses. Onlookers were talking to each other, watching the firefighters, and pointing to her car.

A man swung his young son into his arms and walked away from the scene while two teens rode their skateboards down the sidewalk, expertly dodging anyone in their way.

Her gaze stalled on a man leaning against a brick wall, his arms crossed as though he had all the time in the world. When she took in his face, she was startled to find he was staring right at her. He grinned and tipped an imaginary hat at her before straightening and walking away.

"I see him. Blake, I'll call you back." She ended the call and pressed the button on her earpiece. "We've got a man on the east side of the street heading south." She squinted as she tried to pick up as many details as possible. "Caucasian, gray hair. Wearing dark jeans, a pale blue shirt, and white sneakers. He's passing Phoebe's Finds right now."

Carrington's voice came over the coms. "Moving to intercept."

The suspect ducked down a side street.

"I've lost visual. He turned right on Second Street. Carrington, do you see him?"

She watched as Carrington and Nate met at that corner and then disappeared as they followed the suspect.

A moment later, Carrington spoke again. "Negative. We lost him. Sorry, Durant."

"He had a head start, and I'm sure he had an escape route planned." Jenny sighed in discouragement.

When Nate and Carrington reappeared, Jenny jogged over to join them. "Blake said the bomber has been in contact with him. That he was here and detonated the bomb himself."

Nate walked up and nudged her arm. "Take a look around. There must be at least three security cameras in the area. We'll comb through the security footage and see if we can figure out where he went. Would you recognize him again if you saw him?

"It was the same man from the bar."

Nate spoke into his coms. "Baker, I need you to go around and gather security footage from all the cameras in this area."

"Understood."

He motioned for Carrington to join them.

"I'm going to set up a patrol of the area. The bomber may still be in the area. Take Durant back to the station." Before Jenny could argue, he shook his head to stop her. "I need you to go back and talk to Blake. Find out what he knows. It's a miracle no one was killed today. We need to stop this guy before he adds to the list of fatalities."

Blake paced in front of Lewis's desk while he waited for Jenny to call him back. He wanted to be there with her. To hold her in his arms and reassure himself that she hadn't been injured in the blast. Those few minutes of wondering, not knowing if she was alive or dead, had been some of the most agonizing of his life.

He answered his phone the moment her name popped up on his screen. "Was it him?"

"Yes, but he got away. There are multiple security

cameras up and down this street. Logan's going to go through the security footage once we get a hold of it. With any luck, we'll see where he went or how he fled the scene."

"Did it look like the same guy from the security footage at the bar?"

"Yes, I'm almost certain it was." She gave him a description, which he relayed to Patricia. "We made eye contact, and the way he smiled at me..." She trailed off. "He was glad I spotted him."

Anger flared. The guy was demented and clearly thought this was all a game. The more casualties there were, the bigger the impact his actions had. This was escalating fast. "You need to get off the street, Jenny."

"I know. Carrington's taking me back to the precinct now. You said that the bomber contacted you. What did he say?"

Blake told her about the phone calls. Knowing that this all somehow circled back to him, and that she'd almost died more than once, was enough to nearly crush him. They'd been looking in all the wrong places the last few days. The bomber seemed determined to make Blake pay for something specific. He wished he knew what that was.

"Whoever this guy is, he's getting back at me for something. We're pulling all the cases I've worked where someone was killed, whether by my hand or while I was present. But without more information, it's impossible to know who we're looking for."

"If what he said is true, and he really did plant that bomb on my car days ago, then what was he waiting for?"

Blake squeezed his free hand into a tight fist. "He said he wanted me to know loss. He planned to detonate the bomb while you were in the car so I could watch it go up in flames." He forcibly removed the images from his mind.

A door slammed in the background. "We traveled in the same car while you were here, except for when I drove to the station. He had several perfect opportunities then. So why didn't he trigger the bomb?"

"Maybe he lied when he said how long the bomb had been there. If he intended to detonate it himself, he had to be within sight of your car and close enough to see my reaction. It would've been very difficult to do both in the back parking lot at the precinct."

Torrance rounded the corner and indicated that he needed to speak to Blake.

"Hey, I need to go. Let me know what you guys find on the surveillance tapes. I'll keep you in the loop, too. Be safe."

"I will. You, too."

Blake slipped his phone into his back pocket and turned to Torrance. "The bomber was spotted on the street near the scene. DPD is pulling surveillance footage from surrounding cameras. If we can get a clear image of his face, maybe we'll be able to get an ID."

"Which is why you need to get back down to Destiny."

Blake exchanged a look with Lewis. "What about Caldwell?"

"I've got that case reassigned. Go, but keep us in the loop every step of the way. I don't think I need to tell you to be careful."

"No, sir, you don't. Thank you, sir."

"We'll be monitoring the calls coming into your phone," Patricia told him. "When the bomber calls again, try to keep him on the line as long as possible. I'm going to do my best to get a trace."

"Will do."

Lewis clapped Blake on the back. "I'll keep digging into

past cases. Call as soon as you have more info. And we'll do the same. We're going to get these dots connected."

Blake glanced around the room, thankful that so many people had his back.

He'd be back in Destiny with Jenny in less than two hours. One way or another, he was going to find the bomber and put him behind bars where he belonged.

Chapter Thirty-One

Out of the five different security cameras in the area, only three were functioning. Logan got the footage downloaded to his computer and was busy looking at it in the conference room. Jenny sat nearby with the hope that, between the two of them, they could spot their suspect.

She originally hoped they might have an ID by the time Blake returned to Destiny, but it'd taken much longer than she'd expected to get the security footage in the first place. At least now she could actively do something.

Movement in the doorway caught her attention. She turned to find Blake standing there, a look of relief on his face that she was sure now matched her own.

Without hesitating, she stood and made her way around the conference room table to meet him halfway. He engulfed her in his strong arms and held her tight. Neither of them said a word.

She briefly closed her eyes and allowed herself to breathe in his scent while soaking in his warmth and strength. Reluctantly, they both took a step back.

"I'm glad you're here." She wanted to say so much more.

"Me, too." He studied her face for a moment before turning to Logan. "What've we got?"

Jenny led him over to an empty chair and sat beside him. "We're just now going through the security footage. The first tape didn't have the right angle. But both of the others seem to."

"Good to have you back." Logan gave Blake a nod as he mirrored his computer screen onto the large TV in the room. "This footage is from the sandwich shop you were eating at, Jenny. I'm going to play back the ten minutes before the explosion. See if you recognize the suspect among any of the individuals walking by or standing around."

"He called me right before I called Walker to warn him. So keep an eye out for any men talking on cell phones."

The three of them sat in silence and watched as people strolled down the street. At one point, Nate stepped outside the sandwich shop, closely followed by Jenny and Lisa. The women hugged, and Lisa walked to her car and drove away while Jenny went back inside the restaurant. Minutes later, she returned, gave Nate a wave, and started toward her car as Nate answered his phone.

Jenny knew everything was going to be okay, but she still tensed as the video showed Nate waving at her, closely followed by the explosion that momentarily whited out the screen. Underneath the table, Blake rested his knee against hers.

Logan whistled. "That was way too close for comfort. Okay, keep watching. Let's see if our suspect wanders by after the explosion."

Again, the room became silent until Jenny practically

jumped up from her chair. "I think that's him." Logan paused the video, she hurried around the conference table, and tapped the screen with her finger. "Let's see where he goes."

Instead of returning to her chair, she sat on the edge of the table to one side.

Unlike the rest of the people who were in the area, this man walked calmly through the chaos, his hands tucked into his pockets. He didn't even turn his head to look at the burning wreck of a car and eventually disappeared off the screen.

"That means he had to have been watching from the opposite direction." Blake got up then and came around to stand near Jenny. "Logan, can you pull up a map of the area?"

"Yep, one second." He'd barely spoken the words when a detailed map popped up in a window in front of the security footage. "Here we go."

Blake stepped forward and tapped the restaurant and then the approximate spot where her car had been parked. "So our suspect walks in this direction past the restaurant and your car."

Logan used his computer to indicate the landmarks and then drew an arrow to show the path the suspect had taken.

"Jenny, where did you see him afterward?"

She showed them where she'd seen him leaning against the brick wall. "Then, after he realized he'd been spotted, he walked this way and turned down here."

Logan continued the arrows.

Jenny nodded. "When Baker and Carrington pursued him, they turned that corner and kept going, but he'd disappeared."

"Let's see what angle the other security camera had."

Logan pulled that up and hummed his approval. "It's across the street, but it's farther down." He fast-forwarded the video until the correct time. "Okay, we can't see the restaurant, but you can just see the front of your car here, Jenny."

From this new angle, they could see Jenny dashing away from the car while waving people away. When the car exploded, she fell to the ground.

A few minutes later, they watched as the suspect wandered past her car to lean against the wall. It looked like he was simply enjoying the pandemonium that he'd created.

Logan paused the video again and zoomed in. It wasn't a perfect video by any means, but it was enough to confirm that this man was the same as the one from the bar. "I think this is a better picture than the first. It doesn't hurt to run it through facial recognition again."

He continued the video, and they watched the moment the man noticed that Jenny had seen him. He tipped his invisible hat, turned, and walked out of the frame.

Blake asked Logan to bring the map back up again. "I'd be willing to bet that he had a vehicle parked on the other side of that block. Are there any traffic cams over there?"

Jenny was almost positive there were. If they could get an idea of what kind of car the suspect was driving, they could put out a BOLO. Between having a picture of his face and details about his car, it'd be a lot harder for him to hide.

Blake's phone rang. When he looked at the screen, his back straightened, and he showed it to Jenny. "It's the bomber. The FBI will be trying to trace the location as soon as I answer it. Putting it on speaker." He answered the call. "This is Patterson."

"I see you came to your senses and came back to Destiny. I applaud the gesture, although you should know it'll ultimately do no good."

Jenny's arms broke out in goose bumps. She tried to focus on the suspect's voice.

A muscle in Blake's jaw flexed. "I know you think you're trying to get some kind of vengeance. Without knowing who you are or what you're fighting for, this is all just senseless violence."

"Oh, you'll know who I am. Soon."

The call ended.

A moment later, a text came in from Patricia.

He's within two miles of your location.

Chief Dolman walked into the room. "Where are we?"

Jenny was in the process of updating him when Logan paused the video he was looking through.

"I think I've got something. Here's the suspect coming up Second Street, turning onto Poplar, and getting into a small, four-door car." He paused the recording and zoomed in. "Looks like a navy-blue Jetta."

The chief put a hand on the back of Logan's chair. "Can you see a license plate?"

A few seconds later, they had the perfect shot. "Got it. Running the plate now." He typed the information into another window and waited. "The car was reported stolen in Austin a week ago."

The chief turned to look at Jenny. "Update Detective Walker and get a BOLO out on that vehicle immediately."

"Yes, sir."

Chapter Thirty-Two

They were finally getting the information they'd been looking for to track the bomber down. It was the encouragement that Blake needed because, up until now, their suspect had had the upper hand. At some point, they'd be face-to-face, and Blake intended to know exactly who he was talking to.

The conference room became the central hub for the investigation, and details were listed on a whiteboard as they came in. Logan kept looking at traffic cameras hoping to spot the stolen car again. Blake kept his team in Austin updated, and they continued to comb through old case files looking for possible suspects.

His phone rang, and Lewis's name flashed on screen. "Patterson."

"Hey, man. We went through the old cases that might have left people upset or angry. One in particular stood out. I'm sending it to your phone."

"Okay, hold on. I'm putting you on speaker."

Blake saw the file and forwarded it to Logan and then

put the call on speaker so everyone in the room could hear. He gave Logan a nod.

"We're pulling the case up as we speak. Why did this one stand out?"

"Wade Branson was arrested for dealing. When he was brought in, we discovered that he was tied to a large drug cartel that the FBI and local PD had been working for over a year to eradicate. In exchange for a lighter sentence, Branson agreed to go back into the ring and help obtain enough evidence to arrest the head of the cartel."

Blake nodded. "I remember that case. He had a wife and two little girls that were caught up in the middle of it all." He glanced at Jenny, who was listening intently. "We got a wire on him and sent him to introduce a new buyer in town—an undercover officer. Everything had been pre-arranged, and we had boots on the ground ready to storm in should things fall apart."

Lewis continued the story. "Branson turned on the undercover cop, exposing him to the cartel to prove his dedication. Patterson and I were on the team that stormed the building to retrieve the cop and take Branson back into custody."

"Despite multiple attempts to get Branson to surrender, he pulled out a gun and aimed it at the cop, and I was forced to shoot him." Blake remembered it vividly. There was no way Branson was going to walk away from the situation. It was clearly suicide-by-cop. "He died on the scene."

Blake looked at the picture of Branson that was on the large screen and shook his head. It was all such a waste. The guy was only twenty-five.

"What happened to his family?" The question came from Walker.

Lewis responded. "We took them into protective

custody. She insisted on attending his funeral for the sake of the children, and then they entered WITSEC. If they hadn't, the cartel likely would've had them killed." He paused. "The funeral service was two years ago today."

"That seems like quite the coincidence," Walker commented.

Blake remembered that funeral well. Branson's widow had never blamed him for the death of her husband. As it turned out, she was planning on leaving him so the kids wouldn't be exposed to the kind of life that Branson insisted on living. She'd asked Blake to attend the funeral, and out of respect, he did. Not everyone was happy to see him there.

Especially Branson's father who had confronted Blake at the funeral and told him to leave.

Suddenly, all the other noise in the conference room faded as Blake tried to picture Branson's father. He'd been morbidly obese with scraggly hair and a foul attitude toward Blake and anyone else in law enforcement.

"Patterson, you still there?" Lewis's voice brought Blake's attention back to the phone.

"Yeah, I may have something. Logan, can you bring up the image we have of the bomber from earlier today?"

"Sure." He enlarged it and put it up on the TV.

"Can you do a search for Wade Branson's father? I don't recall his first name, but I know they had the same last."

Logan typed on his computer. "Looks like Wade's mother died when he was five, and he was an only child. His father is Caleb Branson. Last record we have of him is that he resided in Austin, but I'm not seeing much about him since his son's death. Let me see if I can find a photo." It took a few minutes, but he finally found one and put it up on screen along with the image of their bomber.

Blake took a screenshot and sent it to Lewis who was

still on the phone. "Sending the comparison photos to you now."

Everything about the two men was wildly dissimilar from the two-hundred-pound weight difference to the hair. But those eyes and the nose...

"I'm confident we're looking at the same person here," Walker confirmed. "Logan, can you run a facial comparison?"

The older photo showed a man with full cheeks and bushy facial hair. The bomber's face was thin, with loose skin hanging below his chin and was clean shaven. Even still, Blake knew what the answer would be even before Logan's computer blinked with a 100% probability.

"It's a match, Lewis. Our bomber is Caleb Branson."

Logan spoke up again. "According to what I'm seeing here, Caleb had no other family."

"And he blames you for the death of his son," Lewis said over the phone.

Jenny shook her head. "And since his daughter-in-law and his granddaughters entered WITSEC, he may blame you for losing them, too. Essentially, instead of admitting that his son's poor choices led to the breakdown of Caleb's family, he's chosen to hold you responsible."

Blake raked his fingers through his hair and sat on the edge of the conference table. He couldn't imagine allowing that level of hatred to consume him.

He picked up his phone. "Thanks, Lewis."

"No problem. Be careful, Blake. A man like that has nothing to lose."

"Understood." He ended the call and sought out Chief Dolman who was standing at the edge of the room. "Chief, I'd like to officially apologize for bringing this mess to your doorstep."

"While I appreciate that, it's not your fault. It doesn't matter where he came from or why. What matters is that we get him off the street and behind bars where he can't hurt anyone else."

Murmurs of agreement echoed around the room.

Blake was about to thank them for their support when his phone rang again. "It's Branson."

Everyone quickly vacated the room except for Logan, Jenny, the chief, and Walker.

Blake answered and put it on speakerphone. "This is Patterson."

Chapter Thirty-Three

There was a moment or two of silence after Blake answered the phone before Branson finally spoke. "I've been thinking about it, Patterson. You want to know who I am? I want you and Officer Durant to meet me somewhere. No other cops. No more games. I have a list of demands, and if you grant me those, then I may allow your little girlfriend to walk away from this alive." He sounded confident that his plan was moving forward exactly how he wanted it to.

Blake looked at Chief Dolman, who tilted his head as if to say, "go on."

It was time to let Branson know that he no longer had the upper hand.

"I know exactly who you are, Caleb Branson, and you're not in any position to be making demands. You listen to me, and you listen carefully. Killing Officer Durant won't bring your son back, and I'm not going to let you hurt anyone else. The way I see it, you have two choices. You can turn yourself in, or you can run and hide."

There was nothing but silence on the other end of the

call until something like a grandfather clock began to bong in the distance. The call ended abruptly.

Immediately, Jenny moved toward Logan. "That was the clock..."

"...in front of the library," Logan finished.

"It's only two blocks away." Chief Dolman straightened. "I want patrols on the streets looking for that navy-blue Jetta. Check hotel and motel parking lots within hearing distance of the library."

"On it." Walker held his phone to his ear as he left the room.

"I'm checking traffic cameras in the area as well," Logan told them.

Jenny moved closer to Blake. "He's backed himself into a corner now. He's desperate, and that only makes him more dangerous."

She wasn't wrong.

Blake needed to be doing something. Anything. "I'm going to get some more coffee. Do either of you need some?"

Logan barely shook his head, his attention on his computer screen.

"I'll come with you," Jenny volunteered and led the way to the break room.

They were greeted by a pot of freshly-brewed coffee and a surprisingly empty room. She poured him a cup and handed it to him before getting one for herself. They sat down at the small table, and Blake relished the relative quiet.

Jenny took a sip of her coffee. Even though her eyes were alert, she looked exhausted. He wondered if the fall after the explosion had made her knee worse or caused her any additional pain.

Most of all, he wanted to reach across the table for her

hand, but someone could come into the room at any time, and he needed to keep it professional.

Instead, he tapped the toe of her shoe with his and drew in a deep breath. "I'm sorry you got pulled into all of this."

Her eyes widened in surprise. "It sounds to me like this guy would've found a way to make himself heard one way or another. You're not responsible for that."

"Maybe not, but knowing I'm the one who brought trouble right to your doorstep... I'd never be able to forgive myself if something happened to you."

"For right now, let's just pray we have the opportunity to catch this guy and keep everyone else safe. Then, we can go back to worrying about the little things. Like living an hour and a half apart." She smiled then, and there was something about the way the corners of her lips lifted and her eyes sparkled that eased some of the burden from his shoulders.

"I like the sound of that."

A hand slapped the doorframe, and Nate leaned in. "We found the car at a hotel on Teak Boulevard. Carrington and Smith are going in now. Bomb squad is standing by."

Their coffee forgotten, Blake and Jenny followed Nate back to the conference room.

Logan handed them each an earpiece.

Carrington was reporting. "The manager positively identified Branson as the occupant of room seventeen. We're heading that way now. The building is being evacuated as we speak."

Moments later, they heard the officers pounding on the hotel door. "Caleb Branson, this is the Destiny Police Department. Open the door."

Silence.

"Bomb squad is checking the entrance for explosives."

More silence.

"We're cleared to enter. Proceeding with caution."

Blake said a silent prayer for the officers' safety.

Sounds of shuffling and banging came over the coms along with several utterances of "Clear!"

Carrington finally spoke. "Branson isn't here, but we couldn't have missed him by much. There are a lot of supplies that could be used for constructing a bomb, and most of it has been opened or is partially gone. I think we need to clear the hotel and have the bomb squad go through the room to be sure. We're vacating the area now."

"Understood. Good work, officer." Chief Dolman turned to address Walker. "Branson may be on the run. Alert all units to be on the lookout."

"Yes, sir."

Blake's cell phone rang, and he glanced at the screen.

"It's Branson." He let it ring another time or two before answering it and putting it on speaker. "This is Patterson."

"Ding-dong. Since you refused to meet with me, I was forced to come to you. I want you and Durant to come to the main entrance. For everyone listening, don't try to be the hero, or Tia here will be the first to die."

The call ended.

"He's got Tia?" Logan's eyes widened as he got to his feet. "He has to know everyone is looking for him. Coming here is like committing suicide."

"He needs an audience." Blake exchanged a worried glance with Jenny, who was standing nearby, her hands clenched into fists. They weren't going to let Branson hurt Tia or anyone else.

Chief Dolman put a hand on the back of Logan's chair. "Bring up the security feed from the main entrance."

A moment later, two different images came on screen

showing the large waiting area. Caleb Branson was standing right in the center of the room. He had a bulky vest on with a series of wires that connected to a handheld detonator.

He looked straight at one of the cameras and extended his arm.

"That looks like a dead man's switch. Quietly start evacuating the building through the back exit. Now. I want everyone gone except for myself, Walker, Patterson, Logan, and Durant. Call Lorenzo back from the hotel. We're going to need him to diffuse that bomb."

There was a frenzy of activity outside the conference room as people began to evacuate the building. An officer came in with bulletproof vests for Blake and Jenny, which they put on immediately.

"Keep him talking. Keep him calm. We need to evaluate the situation, and we'll be able to do that more accurately once you're down there." Nate looked from Blake to Jenny. "Find out what's on his list of demands. We need time to get as many people out of the building as possible and get Lorenzo back here."

"Understood." Jenny crossed her arms in front of her vest, her hands gripping either side. Her gaze slid to Blake's, and even though there was a hint of worry in her eyes, there was a determination there, too.

Blake's respect for her soared, as did his regret that she was in this position in the first place. "Let's do this."

Together, they walked through the nearly empty halls to the front of the building. Nate was behind them, his weapon drawn.

"I'm staying on this side of the door until we know more about the situation," he told them. "But you've got backup."

Blake opened the first of two locked doors between them and extended his hands. "Branson, we're coming out."

"Make it slow."

Blake did just that, with Jenny close behind him. As they entered the middle area where staff and officers assisted the public from behind bulletproof glass, he counted Tia and three other staff members who were standing against the far wall of the main lobby, their hands at their sides.

Branson was situated in the center of the lobby. Now that they were closer and in person, Blake could see the explosives strapped to his vest. He held the trigger in his hand, and his thumb was pressing firmly down on the red button on the top.

Just as the pictures had suggested, he'd lost a lot of weight. Too much. He looked unhealthy, with his skin sagging and his cheeks sunken in. The last two years had not been kind to him.

Two civilians sat on the floor, their knees to their chests, in front of Branson. They must have been in the lobby when Branson first came in.

"Okay, Branson. We're here."

The man grinned at him and tilted his head. "Come on out here with me. You know very well that bullet-proof glass will do nothing if I decide my hand is getting tired."

That much was true. Blake looked over at Jenny who gave a slight nod.

"We'll come out there, but once we do, I want you to let all these other people go."

"Done."

Jenny gave Tia a firm look and another slight nod.

She opened the outer door, and they stepped into the lobby. Blake held the door open until Branson finally motioned for the two people sitting on the floor to leave.

They got up and hurried through the door. From there, Tia led everyone else out.

At least now, Branson would be solely focused on him and Jenny. They just had to keep him talking until they got everyone else out of the building.

"I get why you're angry with me. But why are you bringing Officer Durant into the middle of this? Let her go, too, and the two of us can talk."

Chapter Thirty-Four

J enny wanted to tell Blake that she wasn't going anywhere. If he had to stand there and face Branson and that bomb, then she was going to do the same. There was no time to figure it out, though, because Branson only laughed and shook his head.

"I'm not letting her go. You took everything from me, Patterson. Everything. I've been watching you for a while, and it's clear that this partner means something to you. You need to understand that if you don't do as I ask, they'll have to pick her up and carry her out in pieces." He lifted the trigger dramatically with a sneer.

Jenny had no doubt that Branson was serious and forced herself to take even breaths and keep herself calm. Nate's voice came through her earpiece. "Great job getting everyone out of there. We've got two-thirds of the building evacuated."

Blake lifted his hands.

"I'm truly sorry for the death of your son. That was not how I wanted that situation to end. We tried everything we could to find a peaceful resolution. When Wade decided to turn his gun on a police officer, we were left with no choice. *I* was left with no choice." He placed a hand against his chest. "I'm truly sorry for your loss. I can only imagine how difficult it was to bury your son."

Branson's eyes flashed. "You have no idea what it's like to have everything—everyone—ripped away from you. The people you work with turned the rest of them against me. Peggy and the girls never would've left if you hadn't forced her to."

Blake had mentioned that Wade's wife and daughters had entered the witness protection program as soon as his funeral was over.

"I never even had the chance to tell them goodbye. That's on you." He pointed with the hand holding the trigger, and Jenny fought not to flinch as the wire connecting it to the bomb stretched. "If I'd had the chance to talk to them, they would've realized that we could still be a family."

Blake's attention never wavered from Branson. "We didn't force Peggy to leave."

"That's a lie."

Jenny took a step forward. "It's not. No one is forced into the witness protection program. It only works if the people who enter it are dedicated to starting a new life. It's a decision that *they* have to make."

Branson's focus switched to her, and she swallowed hard. His hand holding the trigger was beginning to shake. Whether from adrenaline or fatigue, she wasn't sure. Sweat beaded on his forehead.

"Why would she decide to take those girls away from their only grandparent?" His voice came out in a growl.

Jenny thought back on the case details that Blake had shared with them.

"There were men who were angry with Wade. The same men that Peggy had to testify against. I'm sure they didn't care that she was a single mom or that your granddaughters were just little girls. They were the type of men determined to get even. Peggy probably thought taking the girls away was the only way to keep them safe." She took another small step forward.

"Don't push him too hard, Durant." Nate's voice came through coms.

"Then let me talk to her," Branson insisted. "I want to talk to Peggy and my granddaughters."

"I can't do that." Blake's voice was firm. If he was nervous, there was no visual sign of it.

"You'll arrange for a way to speak with them, or I'll blow us all up right here, right now." This time, when he held his hand out, it shook even more.

Jenny swallowed hard. Branson's thumb had to be getting tired of holding that trigger. They couldn't afford for his thumb to slip.

Blake shook his head. "I'm not saying I won't do it, Branson. I'm saying I can't. I have no idea where they are. No one does. There is no way for me to reach out to her."

Branson's face reddened. "You would rather I kill you both right now? Because that's what you're choosing."

Nate spoke in her ear again. "We've got everyone out of the building, and the bomb squad is here. I think we're running out of time. The one thing Branson's been fighting for is out of reach, and he's starting to realize it."

Jenny could practically feel the man's frustration and anger. She took another step forward and held her hands out to make him feel more at ease. "I'm sure Peggy hated taking the girls and leaving. If you're their only grandparent, then it must have been a terrible decision to make. She probably felt trapped between keeping them safe and keeping you in their lives."

From what she understood, Branson had played a large part in getting his son involved in the drug world. Jenny didn't know Peggy, but she imagined the poor woman didn't hesitate to cut all ties with that way of life. There was no way to know for sure, though, and if talking about that possibility helped to calm Branson down, then that's what she was going to do.

Branson's attention again moved to Jenny's face, and there was a flicker of doubt in his eyes.

Did he think she was lying? Or was it doubt about what he'd come to believe as the truth? She wished she knew for sure.

"Jenny's right. I doubt Peggy would've made that choice if she hadn't felt like she had to for the girls' safety."

"Good job, you two," Nate said into coms. "Durant, he doesn't seem to mind that you keep getting closer. Two or three more steps, and maybe you can surprise him and get your finger on that trigger. Patterson, you're going to need to subdue him. There's no margin for error here. When you're ready, Durant, the code word is reunited."

Jenny tried to ignore the sweat that trickled down her back. Was Blake just as nervous? He still looked cool as a cucumber. She prayed that she did, too.

Branson looked from Blake to Jenny as though he wasn't sure what to believe. He still held his arm out some, his hand shaking continuously. His silver hair looked stringy from sweat, and he wiped his other arm across his forehead. "Even if all of that's true, where does that leave me?"

"It leaves you with hope." Jenny took another step forward and prayed that God would keep them safe and that they'd be able to save Branson's life in the process. "You may not be able to contact Peggy and the girls, but she *can* reach out to you. Do you still live in the same house? Have the same phone number?"

He nodded once.

"Then, when she knows that she and the girls are safe, she may try to call you." Jenny shuffled another step closer. She was in reach now. She kept her eyes on Branson's face as she tried to judge the distance between herself and his hand. If her timing was off even a little…

"It's been two years. Surely, she realizes they are safe now," Branson said as he considered the possibility. Hope flashed in his eyes.

For a moment, Jenny thought he might decide on his own to stand down until something shifted in his face, and doubt displaced the hope. They were out of time.

"Branson, listen to me." She spoke calmly. Softly. A direct opposition to what she was feeling on the inside as she braced herself for what was going to happen next. "You don't know what the future holds. Maybe, one day, Peggy will reach out… and you'll all be reunited."

As soon as the last word left her lips, she took a large step forward and brought her hands in on either side of his, clamping down and sliding her thumb over his. Every ounce of focus was on making sure his thumb didn't move as he started to pull away from her.

Blake darted into view, brought his fist back, and landed a punch to Branson's jaw. Like a puppet whose strings had been cut, Branson sagged. Blake caught his body, and together, he and Jenny slowly lowered him to the floor. She kept her hands over Branson's in a vice grip.

Branson's thumb went slack, but still Jenny pressed hers against it. She heard a door slam open and footsteps hitting the floor.

Then Philip Lorenzo and another member of the bomb squad, both dressed in full bomb suits, came into view. They eased onto the floor beside her.

The officer she didn't know spoke calmly. "Okay, I'm going to slowly slide my thumb in and take over the trigger. Easy."

Jenny allowed him to push his thumb under hers, sliding Branson's out of the way until he had full control of the trigger.

"Great job. Now, move away. I've got it from here."

Lorenzo looked up and waved them back with his arms. "Everyone else get out of the room. Disarming this should only take a minute. It's not very sophisticated."

She barely had a chance to move before someone lifted her by the arm, and half dragged her to her feet. *Blake.* Together, they quickly made their way through the first door and then the second, where Nate was waiting for them. He clapped them both on the shoulder. "Nice work, you two."

They were going to vacate the building, but they'd barely cleared the second door when Lorenzo's voice came over coms. "The bomb has been disarmed."

Nate withdrew a set of handcuffs and went to properly restrain Branson before he came to.

The adrenaline that had kept Jenny going for the last few minutes drained away in a rush. She leaned against Blake, who immediately put an arm around her and drew her close.

Jenny raised her chin to find him gazing down at her tenderly.

"Nice reflexes, Durant."

She chuckled. "Nice right hook, Patterson."

He leaned in and pressed a tender kiss to her lips.

A voice broke through their temporary bubble. "Oh, come on, guys. Is this really the place?"

Jenny leaned back and turned to find Nate standing nearby, a big grin on his face. She hadn't even noticed him returning from cuffing Branson.

She hiked an eyebrow at him. "Seeing as I managed to avoid my third explosion of the week, I think bending the rules might be appropriate.

"Fair enough," Nate said with a wink. "Carry on."

Epilogue
Four Months Later

Blake walked up behind Jenny and slipped his arms around her. He nuzzled her ear and breathed in the soft floral scent of her shampoo. Together, they looked at her empty living room. Every shuffle of their feet seemed to echo. Funny how houses always looked so much bigger once all the furniture had been moved out. Right now, Jenny's things were loaded in the trailer out front. They'd worked all day to clean the house so that it wasn't a complete disaster for the new owners to move into next week. All Jenny needed to do now was drop the keys off with the realtor.

He leaned his head forward to kiss her jaw just below her earlobe. "You're absolutely sure about this, right?"

Jenny laughed softly as she turned in his arms to face him. "It's a little too late to change my mind now, isn't it? Our friends spent the whole morning loading the last of my things, and the house is already sold. I don't think there's an undo button for that."

"Did you want there to be?"

They'd talked about their plans extensively. But now

that everything was set in motion, he worried she might be second-guessing things. After all, the changes were easy for him to make. His fiancée was moving to Austin where she was going to live in an apartment for six months before they got married in October. They'd be able to have dinner together most nights, maybe even meet for lunch occasionally, and at least have the same home base if either of them had to travel for work.

It was a much better situation than driving to see each other whenever they could over the last four months.

On the other hand, Jenny was the one who was making huge changes, and all at once. She was moving from Destiny, the town where she'd lived her whole life, and leaving her family behind. She was also taking a lateral transfer to the Austin Police Department. Being a police officer in a big city was going to be very different from what she was used to.

Jenny stood on her tiptoes and wrapped her arms around his neck. "I definitely don't need an undo button."

He gently lifted her chin with a finger until he could see her beautiful brown eyes. "I'm glad." He savored her happy sigh and sent up a silent prayer of thanks that he'd finally found his partner for life.

She kissed him softly before resting her cheek against his chest. "I know it's a lot all at once, but it's all good things. I can always come back here to visit, and Destiny will always be my hometown. But you, Blake, are my home."

Special Thanks

This book was written on a super tight schedule, so I want to thank my family who had to put up with me during that time. Ha! Thank goodness most of my book schedules aren't quite that stressful. I love you guys!

Erynn, you managed to get my book edited in the midst of dealing with Hurricane Helene and my tense writing schedule. Seriously, lady, you are a rockstar, and I appreciate you.

Denny, Steph, and Alice, I'm so thankful for each of you. You take the time to read early copies of each of my books and are always good at finding those typos that seem to sneak through no matter what. Thanks to you, I'm able to release my books at their best.

To the members of my ARC team, you are all greatly appreciated. Thanks for your efforts and encouragement.

Father God, You constantly amaze me with Your unending love and blessings. Thank you for never giving up on me.

About the Author

Melanie D. Snitker is a *USA Today* bestselling author who writes inspirational romance and romantic suspense. She and her husband live in Texas with their two children. They share their home with two dogs and two terrariums filled with small critters. In her spare time, Melanie enjoys photography, reading, training her dog, playing computer games, and hanging out with family and friends.

https://www.melaniedsnitker.com/

Books by Melanie D. Snitker

Danger in Destiny

Out of the Ashes

Frozen in Jeopardy

Beneath the Surface

Caught in the Crosshairs

Running from the Past

In Search of the Truth

Assigned to Protect

Brides of Clearwater

Marrying Mandy

Marrying Raven

Marrying Chrissy

Marrying Bonnie

Marrying Emma

Marrying Noel

Books by Melanie D. Snitker

Love's Compass Complete Series

Finding Peace

Finding Hope

Finding Courage

Finding Faith

Finding Joy

Finding Grace

Love Unexpected Complete Series

Safe In His Arms

Someone to Trust

Starting Anew

Healing Hearts

Calming the Storm

I Still Do

Don't Kiss Me Goodbye

Sage Valley Ranch

Charmed by the Daring Cowboy

Welcome to Romance

Fall Into Romance

A Merry Miracle in Romance

Made in the USA
Columbia, SC
08 January 2025

51390884R00131